THE FOREST
OF FOREVER

THE FOREST OF FOREVER

THOMAS BURNETT SWANN

WILDSIDE PRESS

To **BOB ROEHM,**
my tutelary spirit in the dark weirwoods

THE FOREST OF FOREVER

PART ONE
EUNOSTOS

CHAPTER I

I AM THREE hundred and sixty years old and I pride myself, not unjustly, on having enjoyed twice as many lovers as I have years. I have loved Men, Minotaurs, Centaurs, and Tritons and no one has ever complained that Zoe, the Dryad of Crete, has failed in the art of love. Saffron, the erstwhile queen of the Thriae or Bee-Folk, once called me as weatherbeaten as my oak. She pointed to the gold tooth fitted by my Babylonian lover of twenty—no, thirty summers ago, and to the streaks of gray in my green hair, like moss among leaves. I, in turn, expanded the twin grandeurs of my unsagging breasts.

"My dear," I replied, with more courtesy than she deserved, "who wants a sapling when he can have a full-fledged oak?"

I hardly need to add that in these days when everyone is telling his own history—on papyrus, clay tablets, or palm leaves—I have innumerable stories to tell, and since decorum has never been one of my burdens, I am sorely tempted to tell you about some of my escapades. The Babylonian. The Briton. The Achaean (lusty brute!). The only thing that silences me is the fact that some of my friends—and enemies, for every desirable woman is envied as much as she is desired—have a much more ennobling tale to be told. Since those involved are unable to speak for themselves, I must speak for them. As a matter of fact, I do at times take part in the melancholy events: I participated as well as observed. But I neither claim nor wish to be the heroine, poor, dreaming Kora, who was cursed with beauty as some women are cursed with ugliness. However, I will presume to speak for her, even to some of her thoughts, as well as for Eunostos, the last Minotaur, and Aeacus, the Cretan prince.

I promised you a melancholy tale, but where is the forest without its wells of light? If you demand a death or a rape on every tablet, my story is not for you.

*   *   *   *

Hooves crossed, tail at ease, Eunostos lay on his back in a patch of yellow gagea. He had cradled his head in a deserted ant's nest and he held a reed pen between his teeth. There is nothing more reposeful than a reposing Minotaur calf. His race has a reputation for ferocity and indeed, when aroused, they are fierce and redoubtable warriors—a match for the Centaurs, more than a match for Men. Under ordinary circumstances, however, they are peaceful beings, given to gardening, carpentry, or contemplation.

He was a strapping boy (and I use the word "boy" not in the sense of his being Human but of being young), tall, muscular, though just fifteen; with a ruddily handsome face and a mane of woodpecker-red hair of which he was justly proud.

"Eunostos."

He sat up, twitched his tail, which was tipped with red fur and admirably designed for swatting flies, and dropped the pen from his teeth. I noticed the shapely horns beginning to sprout through his mane. Yes, he would soon be a bull.

"Did somebody call my name?" His voice was deep but the tone was mild. It was the kind of voice which says: Linger and chat. Our talk will be small but satisfying.

I stepped out of the trees. He sprang nimbly to his hooves, crossed the meadow in a quick bound, and caught me in a boyish embrace. It always pleased me to see his admiration: a youngster admiring a woman of experience who has kept her looks through years and vicissitudes. In fact, I was looking my best, as my mirror had told me that morning when I donned my leaf-of-the-water-lily gown, adorned my wrists with bracelets of time-greened copper, and, as a small sacrifice to modesty, emplanted a large tourmaline in the cleft of my bosom.

"Aunt Zoe!" It was a courtesy title which I did not particularly like. I was not his aunt, merely a friend of his deceased mother, who had insisted on the title. (Once upon a time—was it forty years ago?—I had been his father's friend.)

"Eunostos, I'm carrying a basket of acorns to Myrrha and Kora. I thought you might like to join me. That roguish Centaur Moschus has given me no end of trouble since we stopped keeping company and—well, it's good to have a man on hand." I was not in the least afraid of Moschus; I rather enjoyed his importunities and intended to resume keeping company with him—after several reassuring interludes with younger men. (You understand that by "men" I mean male adults of any race, and not necessarily Humans.) But I wanted to make Eunostos feel mature and confident. Orphaned for a year, he badly needed the encouragement and guidance of an older woman.

At the mention of Kora, the prettiest Dryad in the Country of the Beasts, he did not have to be urged.

We started through the woods, Eunostos ahead of me like a good scout, thrashing a suspicious looking thicket, prodding for poisonous serpents with a pointed stick while clutching his reed pen and palm leaf tablet with the other hand. (Yes, Minotaurs have hands; it is only their legs that are hooved.)

"What were you dreaming about when I surprised you, Eunostos?"

"Kora," he confided. "I was writing a poem to her." A shy pleasure illumined his face; his eyes were wide and green and they looked as if they had drunk their color from the sea, though he had never left the forest.

"What about?"

"Love."

"What do you know about love, little one?" The term was relative. He was six feet tall, but his full growth would include another foot.

"But that's what it means to be a poet. You make up what you don't know. Do you think the author of *Hoofbeats in Babylon* had ever been to Babylon?" He began to read from the palm leaf clutched in his hand:

"A Minotaur with gainly hoof
Pursued a Dryad girl.
She spied him from her barky roof
And spruced a wayward curl."

"Don't you mean 'ungainly'?"

"No, this hoof was very nimble." He looked down at his own hooves and stamped them, one after the other, lightly on the turf.

"Promising," I said, "but it needs a bit of polish." What else can you tell a budding poet, if you happen to be unable to distinguish poetry from doggerel?

"What's this, giving me the slip, my girl?" A Centaur bestrode our path; he looked quite awesome with his four legs and two arms and his billowing gray mane. But it was only Moschus, who was no more awesome than a deflated wineskin. A small pig, a pink little fellow a long way from becoming a hog, frolicked between his legs.

"No, Moschus, but I have more to do than dally with you in the forest. I'm on my way to Myrrha's house."

"Who said anything about dalliance? It was conversation I had in mind. And possibly lunch," he added, eyeing the acorns, which Centaurs prize almost as much as Dryads. He looked Eunostos up and down. "Hello, young fellow. How goes the wenching, heh?"

Eunostos nodded courteously and between them there flashed the unspoken comradeship of horned, tailed Beasts; though the Centaurs secretly consider themselves superior because they have six limbs instead of four. Also—and I am not speaking out of conceit—there was the tacit understanding of males who appreciate a desirable woman, with a touch of envy on the part of Moschus, who had temporarily lost me, and a touch of pride on the part of Eunostos, who had temporarily found me, even if in the guise of an aunt.

"Watch out in the forest," Moschus called after us, his breath smelling of beer. "There've been—portents."

Portents? What kind? I wish I had paused to question him. But he is something of a wiseacre and a pause would have given him a chance to retell one of his limited and long-winded anecdotes.

"I hope he won't step on his pig," muttered Eunostos. "I've just thought of a new poem:

> *Piglet,*
> *Minikin-flanked*
> *And deft to root and dig,*
> *By what mischance do you expand*
> *To pig?"*

We continued our trek, glimpsing a Bear Girl as she peeped shyly at us from the bushes, watching a blue monkey turn somersaults over our heads. In the Country of the Beasts, there was life at every turn of a path. We, the Beasts—that is, those beings like Centaurs, Minotaurs, and Dryads who combine the attributes of Men with those of the lower animals—hunted birds and rabbits for food (never for sport), but we did not hunt each other; thus, at least at that time, there was little reason for caution or concealment. I do not mean to say that there were not any dangers; there are vipers and vampire bats and occasional wolves—and the Panisci or Goat Boys were notorious thieves. But, generally speaking, the Bear Girls hid and peeped and vanished only because they were shy.

Our country, our forest, was not like other forests. Oak and cypress and elm, tamarisk and cedar, copses and meadows and wooded knolls: these you could find in many places on Crete. But you see we dwelt with our forest, we never tried to master her, wound her, crush her to our purposes. We never cut down the trees to make our houses; we simply borrowed a few limbs from overluxuriant elms, or reeds from the river bank, and built among the trees. We trod the narrowest of paths and never made roads because we did not like to crush the vegetation under our feet. The forest was our home, but we were its guests and not its masters. It was still our happy time.

> *"The Minotaur has combed his mane,*
> *The girl has left her roof—"*

He paused. "What rhymes with 'mane'?"

"Bane," I said without thinking.

"But that's such a gloomy word, and this is a happy poem. The girl is going to requite him, you know."

"I'm sorry, Eunostos. I guess I was thinking about Moschus's portents." Also, though I did not tell him, I was suffering a presentiment of danger without in the least guessing its nature. It is both the blessing and the curse of Dryads that they can sometimes foresee the future, but cloudily, as if they were peering from the surface at the bottom of a muddy stream and trying to distinguish the form of rock and snail and fish.

The first portent came in the shape of a sudden storm. There was a clap of thunder; the recently cloudless sky hurled down a wrath of rain. Even under the oak trees we were drenched; the water collected above our heads till it weighed down the branches and then it poured onto us in torrents. Eunostos's hair was matted to his head, exposing his horns in all of their red-tinted ivory. My water-lily-leaf gown enveloped me like a clammy snakeskin and the leaves threatened to separate and reveal my ample splendors.

"Well, it's not quite a disaster," I said. "We can dry off at Kora's house. I guess Moschus's portent had to do with the weather."

But the storm had brought more than rain. A great black

cloud lingered above our heads even when the rest of the sky had cleared. Suddenly we saw that it was composed of individual segments, entities, beings. It was not a cloud but a flock of what seemed to be enormous birds.

"By the breast of the Mother Goddess," Eunostos swore. Since the death of his parents, he had picked up such oaths from running with loose company. Since I ran with the same company, I was not affronted. "We're being invaded by vultures."

"No," I said. "I don't think they're vultures. They're not black, not all of them anyway. See, there's a blue one, and red, and green. They seem to be wearing garments and I think they're—yes, I know they are."

"What?" he asked, deferring to the accumulated experience of my three hundred and sixty years.

"Thriae."

"Bee-Folk?" he cried. "From the mainland?"

"Yes," I said. "The bright ones are the queens and drones. The dark ones are the workers. The storm must have blown them off their course. Or maybe they're searching for a new home."

"They aren't very nice, are they?" His tail twitched as if assailed by flies.

"I've never met any myself, but the Centaurs say that they're given to thievery and other petty practices. Whether they're capable of worse, I don't really know."

The Thriae circled above us, chattering in high melodious voices (the queens and drones) or guttural monotones (the workers) and no doubt deciding where they should land. It was not long before they had divided into six swarms, each with its own queen, and one of the swarms appeared to be heading straight for us. I hurried Eunostos among the trees, but I turned and looked over my shoulder and directly into the face of a queen, hovering like a monstrous dragonfly a few cubits above my head. She was not looking at me, however; she was looking at Eunostos as if—well, as if he were the chosen drone in her nuptial flight.

"Come on, Eunostos," I said quickly, to keep him from looking over his shoulder and into the naked face of lust. "Whatever they're up to, it's nothing good. Let's warn Myrrha and Kora."

The house of Myrrha, as befitting that of a Dryad whose deceased husband and most of whose lovers had been Centaurs, was an oak tree whose trunk opened into a circular reed cottage on the ground. The reeds were painted a vivid green to match the leaves of the tree. There were two windows, framed by red clay, and a very tall doorway whose door was the skin of two wolves so skillfully stitched together that they might have belonged to one tremendous animal. There were no defenses except removable parchment in the windows, a precaution against the blasts of winter winds or the foragings of vampire bats. When you entered the cottage, you could climb the circular stairs inside the trunk to the upper room, also constructed of reeds, and lodged among the branches like a bird's nest, though much more tidy and trim.

Myrrha was downstairs seated at her loom and weaving a tapestry embroidered with a flattering likeness of her late husband (presumably Kora's father). As conceived by his widow, he embodied the noblest attributes of his race: strength, wisdom, and lustiness. Myrrha herself was fragile without being peaked: a thin, gracefully aging woman whose green hair had turned to silver and whose ears were as delicate as murex shells. Surprisingly, in view of her appearance, she had enjoyed more lovers than anyone else in the country except me. Perhaps her success lay in the fact that she said yes when she looked as if she would say no.

"Myrrha, I've brought a guest," I boomed.

"Zoe and Eunostos," she trilled. "Kora, come down at once, we have visitors." She motioned me to a bench against the wall, where I sank in a heap of cushions and rested my aching feet (I am not plump, you understand; the weight of my bosom places an undue strain on my ankles).

"Here," I said. "I brought you some acorns."

She accepted the gift as if they were emeralds from the land of the Yellow Men. "My dear, what a feast! My tree isn't bearing well this year. We'll roast them tonight. But you're wet to the bone. And you too, Eunostos. Slip into one of my robes, Zoe, while I rub Eunostos down with a cloth." Eunostos, of course, was naked, like all young Beasts and many old ones.

"Thriae," Eunostos announced, beginning to glow beneath a brisk massage. "Right here in the forest. Zoe and I saw them arrive with the storm."

Myrrha dropped the cloth. "Bee-Folk! You don't say." She began to ruminate about the perfidy of the race, the mischief we must expect. Myrrha was notorious for her ruminations. It was said of her that if you wanted to make an announcement to every Beast in the forest, you should whisper it to Myrrha and swear her to secrecy.

At this point, Kora descended the stairs. She walked so quietly that it was the bark-and-leaf scent rather than the sound which announced her coming. She was tall and slender without being thin, rather like a white lotus, it seemed to me, and her beauty was of the sort which soothes rather than excites. To look at her was like dipping hot, tired ankles into a cool stream.

Eunostos deftly retrieved the fallen cloth, rolled over the floor to Kora's feet, and tossed her the cloth. She smiled indulgently down at him, the smile of a young woman for a mere lad of fifteen, and, avoiding his flanks, proceeded to dry his mane.

"Queens, workers, and drones—we saw them all," he said, gazing up at her with adoration.

"Never mind about the drones," said Myrrha. "They're good-for-nothing sluggards who loll in the hives or under the trees. It's the women you have to watch. I heard about them—the queens, that is—from my late husband. They'll snatch the threads from your loom if you give them a chance."

"The drones must do something," suggested Eunostos. "Or the queens wouldn't keep them around."

Myrrha raised a reproving eye at him. Like many free-living women, she was prudish in the company of her daughter. "As I said, it's the queens who are the trouble-makers. I wonder what they want in the Country of the Beasts. We have so little for them to steal."

"I expect the storm blew them here by accident," I said. "Let's hope they don't stay."

We soon turned to other subjects. Happy subjects, on the whole, though it always saddened me to visit the home of two menless women. Myrrha still enjoyed frequent, if itinerant, lovers, but Kora at eighteen was the oldest virgin in the country and a cause of concern for her mother.

Since I myself was a trifle old for Eunostos, I had resigned myself to yielding him to Kora. In fact, I was quietly engineering their union, since he was the last Minotaur and it seemed to me that Kora, once cured of her virginity, could bear him noble sons. You understand, of course, that the offspring of a Minotaur and a Dryad are not hybrids: the sons are Minotaurs, the daughters are Dryads. There are several races in the Country of the Beasts, but each race is either male or female with the sole exception of the Centaurs, who have their own females but also enjoy the women of other races. Humans have questioned why the Great Mother created so many races with a single sex and compelled them to mingle if they wished to multiply. The answer is clear: she likes variety. She likes for opposite to attract opposite. She wants her many-faced, many-figured children to value difference as well as familiarity.

"Now you must have some wine and honey cakes. Will blackberry do?"

"Admirably."

"You may have a cup, too, Eunostos. My, aren't you the young bull now!" (I did not tell her that, since he had been orphaned, Eunostos never drank milk when he could get wine, and much preferred beer; it came of his running with loose company.) "When I finish this robe for Kora, I must weave you a loin-cloth." She fetched a flagon from her cupboard and proceeded to fill some wooden mugs.

"My husband carved them," she said, "and I wouldn't change them for silver."

The clay oven glowed; the scent of raisin-eyed cakes pervaded the room; hospitality was a tangible presence, like a Centaur's pet pig. I did not even hear the dripping of the water clock. How could I know that it was the last peaceful time the four of us were to spend together?

"Eunostos, will you see me home?" I finally asked, when the parchment in the windows no longer glowed with the afternoon sun.

By this time Eunostos was quoting a poem to Kora, and Kora was listening with a faint appreciative smile; but I had the oddest feeling that it was not Eunostos she heard.

CHAPTER II

EUNOSTOS STOOD at the foot of Kora's tree and debated if he should call her name. If he knocked at the door in the trunk, Myrrha would answer and inflict an interminable monologue on him before she called her daughter from the upper room. Beside him was his friend Partridge, the Paniscus, who lent him advice and support. Partridge was thirty. Like all of his race of Goat Boys he had failed to develop, both physically and mentally, beyond the age of fifteen; but in Partridge's case, mentally at least, it was closer to twelve. He was plump, hairy, and sandy from the warren in which he lived; thistles stuck to his flanks and his breath reeked from the stalks of onion grass he was even now nibbling. But Eunostos loved him because Partridge was something of an outcast among his own people, being rather too fat for their rough and tumble ways and too gentle to like those ways even had he not been fat.

Between them, eyeing the tree and catching vibrations with his feelers, crouched Bion, the Telchin, a three-foot, antlike being who lived under the ground, cut gems with his metal-hard pincers, and made bracelets and rings, anklets and necklaces, as well as various beauty aids like kohl and carmine, which he traded to the Dryads and Bear Girls in return for hazelnuts and wheaten bread. He was much more intelligent than a monkey or a cat, though rather less than a Beast. To Eunostos he was, like Partridge, a friend.

"Go on," nudged Partridge. "Call her." He munched furiously on his onion grass.

"Kora." It was less a call than a whisper.

"Eunostos, give her a good bellow."

"*KORA,* I've come to visit." He brandished a spray of violets and peered hopefully at the porch which circled the trunk and the upper room.

A leather door-hanging rustled to the side and Kora appeared on the porch. Her gown of green linen was embroidered with white narcissi, and her face was white, too, like the unveined marble which has lain in the earth since the Great Mother lived on the island, before the coming of Men and Beasts. Her hair, the color of ivy in sunlight, tendriled about her shoulders. She wore neither rings nor anklets nor bracelets, but only a pendant around her neck: a Centaur of hammered silver which she presumed to be a likeness of her father. It was not a single attribute, however, which caught Eunostos's eye; it was an aura of remoteness, of inviolability. She was like an unexplored cave or a silent underground river: secret and alluring and a little frightening.

At eighteen, she seemed to Eunostos decidedly an older woman and therefore the more to be desired. Had she not been beautiful, she might have been called a spinster. (Yes, we have them, poor things, even in the Country of the Beasts, along with a delightful number of rakish bachelors.) As it was, she had often been called aloof, disdainful, and frigid—but never undesirable. In truth, she was none of these things. She was simply waiting. For what, she could not have told you.

"Eunostos," she called down to him. "Have you come to call on mother?"

"I've come to call on you." It was his first such admitted call, though ostensibly he had visited her mother Myrrha often during the past few months, in spite of the fact that she was as garrulous as a sparrow at sunrise. "This time you come down to me."

His tail lashed furiously; he was very nervous.

She hesitated. She's heard those stories about my wenching, he thought, not without a certain pride. At fifteen, it is pleasant to be thought a sly young rogue.

"Very well."

Eunostos was grateful that she did not linger coquettishly in her tree to change her robe or sweep a tortoiseshell comb through her hair. She never seemed aware of her own beauty, except as a kind of nuisance which brought uncountable Centaurs, from striplings right up to senile old Moschus, to knock at her tree. In six twinklings of a firefly, she emerged from the door at the foot of the tree.

"Give her the flowers," hissed Partridge, so concerned for his friend that you could forgive him his onion breath and thistled flanks. He was none too bright but he knew what to do when a Dryad stood in her doorway. For that matter, Eunostos knew what to do with the more accessible Dryads. My friend Myrtle had taught him the facts of life when he was eleven. For the last year, he had been an orphan, knocking about the woods on his own, making his home in caves and warrens or under trees, living it up with the young Centaurs and making free with the Dryads, but somehow never forgetting the manners, the innate gentleness, taught to him by his own Dryad mother and his Minotaur father.

He presented the flowers and Kora took them from his hand. His tail made furious swishes and he stamped his hooves from sheer nervous tension.

The violets had started to wilt—he had held them too long and too tightly in his big hot fist—but Kora received them as if they were roses. She said little; she rarely said much. Stillness seemed to envelope her like a wedding garment (for Beasts thought of weddings, not orgies, when they courted Kora, just as they thought of orgies not weddings when they courted her mother or me). But she smiled and touched him affectionately on his horns.

"Dear Eunostos. They're lovely." She was being tactful; Dryads hate to see any vegetable life uprooted, cut, and otherwise mutilated. We would rather leave flowers on their bushes and bushes in the ground. If we eat acorns, it is only to keep them from the squirrels and to give us energy when we depart from our oaks.

Impulsively he seized her hand and drew her after him with an irresistible tug. She dropped the violets, the wind spread her hair and billowed her ankle-length gown, and she burst into sudden laughter.

"You laugh like wind chimes," Eunostos said. "The ones the Centaurs hang in their windows."

"Was I laughing?" she asked. "I didn't even notice."

Why couldn't she have said, "I was laughing because I am glad to be with you"? But that was Kora, utterly artless and therefore supremely artful.

"Where are we going, Eunostos?"

"To a secret place."

Bion started to follow them; with his eight legs, he could easily have matched their pace. But Partridge stopped him with a loud bleat.

"Don't, you idiot. They want to tryst." Partridge did not have a woman, but his plump body concealed a generous romantic soul, and he liked to imagine his friends in an endless drama of amorous adventures.

Bion lowered his feelers and started to sulk. Telchins can understand our simpler words and "idiot" had stuck in his craw. Partridge patted him on his metallic flank.

"I didn't mean idiot, I meant simpleton," he apologized. His own vocabulary was limited and he supposed that "simpleton" indicated a simple rather than a stupid creature. Fortunately, the word was new to Bion, who appeared mollified. Together they took up a vigil under the tree to await the return of their friend.

Eunostos led Kora along paths between cypress trees and through copses where rabbits stared at them with more curiosity than fear and blue monkeys scampered in search of grubs. Once, they surprised a Paniscus who had turned a tortoise onto its back and was poking it with a stick. Eunostos seized the stick and righted the poor animal and sent him toddling to safety. The Paniscus, whose name was Phlebas, shouted an obscenity and Eunostos flung him onto the grass with a butt to his midriff.

"Grapes that aren't picked shrivel into raisins," Phlebas shouted after them; but Eunostos was too happy to puzzle over the metaphor.

In a blackberry thicket, a Bear Girl dropped her pail and started to follow them. She had no need for clothes or adornments: there was fur on her head that looked like a small round cap through which her ears protruded like jaunty feathers, fur on her body which might have been a winter coat, and a round fur tail like a large hazelnut. But she did at least wear a chain of black-eyed Susans around her neck. Eunostos, though he liked the Bear Girls, did not like being followed at such a time.

"I saw a ferocious bear in the cypress grove," he said. It was enough to send her flying for refuge. Though the Girls claim descent from the goddess Artemis and a gentle brown bear, they insist that later bears, forgetting that notable union, have come to regard them as a rare delicacy. (However, there are no recorded instances of a Girl being devoured by anything but a wolf; it takes a strong stomach to digest so much fur.)

Finally they came to a clearing and a huge tree trunk which had once belonged to the largest, oldest tree in the forest. It was Eunostos's former home, which a year ago had been blasted by lightning. It was then that Eunostos had lost his parents and, as far as we knew, he had not lived in that sorrowful place since their death.

"But Eunostos," Kora cried. "You've cut away all the burned branches and left just the lower part of the trunk. It looks like a small round fort. It was one of those trees left over from the time when the Titans lived on Crete, wasn't it? Everything grew bigger then. Are you living here now?"

"Not yet," he said mysteriously. "Come inside," and he led her through a door, which swung on a wooden hinge, and they stepped inside the trunk. It was roofless and hollow, of course, and on one side he had planted a vegetable garden, where carrot stalks stood like palace guards and cabbages lolled like plump eunuchs, and on the other side, flowers—wild roses and columbine—were the kings and queens of the place.

"But how lovely!" Kora said. "And a little house between the two gardens!" It was a simple round hut with bamboo walls, but so graceful that Kora must have wondered how a seemingly awkward boy could have bent the bamboos to the shape of a peaked crown and cut the windows to look like crescent moons and the door, a great half moon. In the first room, a fountain bubbled out of a pool in the clay floor and cooled the air like a breeze from snow-haired Mt. Ida. There were gemstones on the sandy bottom, gifts from Bion—cornelian, amethyst, beryl—and a little fortress made of seashells which Eunostos had dug from the earth, relics of a time when the Great Green Sea had covered a part of the forest.

"A turtle lives in the fort," said Eunostos. He admired turtles: they were so self-contained—so like Kora and unlike himself.

Nor had he neglected the practical necessities of day-to-day living. After all, the chief characteristic of the Minotaur is that he has an eye for beauty but a hoof for hard work (call him an artisan instead of an artist, if you will; but thus he avoids the overpreciousness of the mere aesthete). Close to the fountain, but out of its spray, was a cross-legged bamboo chair with pillows.

"Zoe sewed the pillows," he confessed, "though I stuffed them." He knew that Dryads liked pillows stuffed with moss, which otherwise encumbered their trees.

"There's also a couch," he added somewhat tentatively, lest Kora suspect him of dishonorable intentions. "In the next room." It was made of wolfskin stretched over a bamboo framework and raised on sturdy hooves. "And a red-brick hearth and cooking pots and, see, a well-stocked larder!" He pointed to a jar of roasted acorns, a tray of snails soaked in olive oil, a cheese of bear's milk, a basket of delicate sparrow eggs, and a weasel pie. "Zoe made the pie. I'm no cook. I hope you are."

"Eunostos, I love your house."

"Our house," he corrected. Surely she can cook, he told himself. Zoe must have taught her.

Kora said nothing. She sat down in the chair and hid her face in a pillow and began to cry. Her tears were silent but very copious.

Eunostos, who was not used to tears, especially from the reticent Kora, knelt beside her and lifted her hair and kissed her on the tip of her pointed ear. It is a Dryad's most sensitive area and only someone who loves her takes such a liberty.

"You don't like my house," he said without reproach. "It's too small, too rustic. It comes of my being an orphan, I expect. I don't have taste."

"Your house is delightful."

"Then it's me. I'm too rough for you. My hooves are dirty, my mane needs trimming."

She stared up at him with eyes so green that even her tears could not keep them from looking like malachites. "No, Eunostos. It's none of those things."

"I'm too young for you then? Callow and inexperienced? But I've been on my own for a whole year now, and orphans grow up fast. I've"—and a note of pride crept into his voice, while his chest expanded by at least three inches—"I've been wenching with the boys."

"I know you've been wenching with the boys. Do you think my mother doesn't tell me such things? You needn't apologize."

"I wasn't exactly apologizing," he stammered.

"I don't hold it against you. What's a young bull to do when he hasn't any family of his own?"

"If I'm not too rough and I'm not too young—"

"You haven't said anything about love."

"But I've shown you how I feel. Isn't that the same thing?"

"A Dryad likes to be told."

"I love you, Kora."

"Why do you love me, Eunostos?"

"Because—because you're beautiful."

"In five hundred years I'll be an old crone."

"And I'll be an old dotard like Moschus, so I don't expect I shall notice."

"I haven't Zoe's bosom."

"You'll develop."

"How much do you love me?"

"More than my new house. More than my friends Partridge and Bion."

"I should hope so."

"More than any other Dryad in the forest!"

"Even Zoe?" (The bitch! And I had cooked the pie for her and sewn the linen pillows.)

He deliberated. (I will have to say that for him.) "I love Zoe very much. Like an aunt and a friend at the same time. But yes, I love you more."

"Go on..."

"Enough to go to work for you! Did you know that there's a trapdoor in the garden which leads to an underground work-shop? That's where I made the chair and couch. That's where I'll make furniture for a livelihood. Kora, I'm going to be a carpenter!"

"That's very nice for you."

"But not for you?"

"Somehow carpentry is not very—poetic." (I would have slapped her.)

"Have some acorns," he said in desperation while he wracked his brain for a poem, and one which he had written to another Dryad, another year, flashed into his mind. Sentimental, to be sure; but Dryads, it seemed—females in general, experience had taught him—thrived on sentiment. It was about a sea-bird instead of a forest bird, but perhaps it would suffice for a moment.

> *"A halcyon is my love,*
> *Who nested on the sea,*
> *But when I raised a silken net*
> *My love eluded me.*
>
> *"A halcyon is my love,*
> *Who nested on the sea,*
> *But when I lifted open hands*
> *My love came down to me."*

"Dear Eunostos. No one has ever written me such a charming poem!"

"Then you'll share my house with me?"

"You *are* offering marriage, aren't you?"

"We'll have the biggest wedding in the country. Zoe will play her flute and Moschus will lead the Dance of the Python. All the Centaurs will come, and the Bears of Artemis, but only Panisci like Partridge who know how to hold their beer. What do you say, Kora?"

She turned away from him and wandered among the delicacies of his meticulously stocked kitchen and returned to the room of the fountain. For a long time she stared into the water.

"Not yet, Eunostos. I'm still waiting."

"But Kora, for what?" Her evasions were maddening him.

"I don't know," she said. "I have these dreams, you see. Of places beyond the Country of the Beasts. Palaces and people, dragon-prowed ships and big beautiful wagons covered with painted canopies and drawn by animals that look like the bottom part of Centaurs."

"Horses." He had read *Hoofbeats in Babylon*.

"And right here on Crete, ladies in great belled skirts, and men who wrestle bulls—"

"Personally," said Eunostos, "I don't think it's very nice to wrestle with bulls, and keep them penned up, and maybe kill them for beef."

"The Cretans don't kill them. At least not in the ring. It's a kind of ritual. Men and bulls perform together. It's an honor for the animals, who are considered sacred to the gods. And the Men are very valiant and agile."

"Oh," he said, reassured about the bulls. "And these are the things you want?"

"I can't be sure until I see them for myself."

"Are you thinking about taking a trip? Like the Centaurs when they build their rafts?"

"How far do you think I could get from my tree?"

"You could build a raft out of oak trees." It was worse than a slip of the tongue; it was a desecration.

"And *murder* all those trees? No, I shall just have to wait here in the country until something comes to me."

"Well, a bull isn't coming, you can be sure of that. At least not the wrestling kind." (Foolish Kora, he wanted to cry, can't you see that another kind is right here in the house with you?) "Let's go into the garden." He was not given to long conversations. Pen and palm leaf in hand, he waxed eloquent. But with speech he could be as inarticulate as Partridge, at least in the company of Kora. It was time for another gesture. The violets had wilted but there were roses and columbine.

"No, Eunostos," she cried as he bent to pick a large bud on the verge of opening into crimson opulence. "Let it grow. That way it will live for days. Otherwise, you'll kill it."

He stood up without the rose. "I can't give you anything, can I?" He wanted to recite the poem he had written especially for her—"A Minotaur with gainly hoof..."—but the words stuck in his throat. "I'll just have to wait till I grow older. When I'm sixteen and you're nineteen, the difference between us won't seem quite so great. Whatever you say, the difference does make a difference."

She touched his horns and smiled with infinite sweetness. "I can't expect you to wait for me, Eunostos."

"I don't mind." He thought of the yielding Dryads, wreathed in leafy fragrances and soft as their nest-like couches, who had come into his arms with cries of anticipation and left him with sighs of gratitude. "Eunostos, how did you learn so much so fast? Moschus is four hundred and he could take lessons from you!" Pliant Dryads. Grateful Dryads. Could he forego such delights for as long as a year? Perhaps. At fifteen, anything seems possible (and an occasional lapse, forgivable).

"But don't you see, my dear, in the meantime I may find what I'm waiting for."

"I'll take my chances."

A shadow fell between them and the sunbright flowers suddenly lost their color. They looked up into the sky and Kora cried:

"Eunostos, who is that lovely woman with wings? She must be one of the Bee queens you were telling us about!"

"She looks skinny to me," he said. "And she has no right to spy on us, even if she is a queen!"

"I think she was spying on you," said Kora as the queen dipped above them and vanished over the rim of the tree trunk. "She almost seemed to be—measuring you."

Was there a hint of jealousy in her voice? At any rate, she took his arm as they left the trunk and headed for her tree. It was a liberty which she had accorded to no other male except her presumed father. Of course, thought Eunostos, she may be treating me as a younger brother. On the other hand—

The eyes of the forest watched them with surprise and speculation. The Bear Girl emerged from asylum among the roots of a tree and, regardless of bears, stared after them and spilled the blackberries out of her pail. Phlebas gave a knowing "ha" as he skulked behind a plane tree. Had the grape been plucked?

Partridge and Bion were still idling at the foot of Kora's tree. Kora's mother had invited them to join her for catnip tea, but she boiled her leaves until there was little nip in them, and Partridge was not much for listening to long-winded monologues unless you bribed him with beer. He had declined the invitation with the unarguable excuse that he was not dressed for calling.

"And?" he cried when Kora was in the tree and a slightly bemused Minotaur stood at his side. "The way she was holding your arm, you must have reached an understanding."

"I'm going to wait," said Eunostos.

"Wait! How long?"

"I don't know. A year maybe."

Partridge stamped his hoof angrily and tore a hole in the turf. "These virgins. Give me a willing Dryad any day." (Poor Partridge. All Dryads were unwilling with him.)

"I'm through with wenching," said Eunostos, but not without a certain wistfulness.

CHAPTER III

KORA AWOKE when the sun slanted across her face like the soft creepers of a morning glory vine. She touched her feet to the mossy floor, found her sandals, and lifted a green linen gown from a chest of cedarwood and a cloak which seemed to be woven from pink and white rose petals. She bathed her face from a bowl of rainwater trapped among the branches; she did not bother to look in her mirror, for she had slept peacefully, even if dreamfully, and knew that she had not mussed her hair enough to require a comb.

She walked onto the porch and looked around her at the garden of foliage which enfolded the room like the hand of a friendly Cyclops.

"Father tree," she whispered. "I am going to buy Eunostos a gift." She always spoke to the tree before she left on her day's errands, and the tree shuddered with the pleasure of a stroked animal. She had his consent. He liked Eunostos. Reentering the room, she descended the staircase in the hollow trunk and paused at her mother's couch to look down at the frail, sleeping figure who, having entertained a Centaur during the night, would doubtless sleep until noon. Poor mother. She bad no dream to accompany her; she had to rely on earthier companions.

She opened her arms to embrace the morning, her only lover, with its sunbeams and fragrances, its grass besprinkled with dew like mica. Her reverie was broken by a tapping above her head. Woodpeckers had started to peck at the limbs of her tree. She hurled an acorn at the rowdy birds. Other birds were welcome: swallows and nightingales. But the woodpeckers wounded her tree-father with their cruel beaks.

Eunostos's proposal yesterday had deeply touched her. Not that she meant to accept; not that she wished to encourage him in his pursuit of her. At the same time, she did not wish to discourage him. She could hardly envision a better husband. Gentle yet strong; reasonably faithful; a poet to compensate for also being a carpenter. But did she want a Minotaur for a husband, she who had dreamed of cities and palaces and nimble young Cretans wrestling bulls?

Thus, she must find Eunostos a handsome but not too personal gift. The gift of a sister, not of a lover. What then? The Bears of Artemis were celebrated for their necklaces of black-eyed Susans and they picked raspberries for market, but the thought of Eunostos adorned with black-eyed Susans made her smile and he could surely pick his own berries. The Panisci, rascally youngsters, were totally unproductive. The Telchins hammered metal and set stones for men as well as women, but she could not imagine a ring on one of Eunostos's big fingers. Had he wanted such a ring, or silver tips for his horns, which had been fashionable in his father's day, Bion would long since have made them. The Centaurs then, the practical, agricultural Centaurs, who produced most of the food staples for the country—grain, olive oil, and milk—and all of the farm implements, like rakes and mattocks and bull-tongue ploughs. Since Eunostos had shown her his garden, she would buy him a mattock or hoe (somehow a bull-tongue plough seemed inappropriate for a Minotaur, as well as too large for so small a garden).

But remembering last night's dream, she forgot Eunostos. Dream? No. She had seen too clearly, remembered too vividly. Every night now, it seemed, her soul went out from her body and returned with visions of terror and wonder. Wonderful indeed last night, and a little terrible. She had seen a young prince beside a pool of blue lotuses and silver fish. She had watched him speak to a girl with painted nipples—a brazen girl, to be sure—and then she had followed him as he fled from the palace and took refuge in a grove of tamarisk trees.

She had tried to call to him but she had not even known his name. Still, he had seemed to hear her. He had ardently embraced a tamarisk tree and her own body had throbbed with a sweet anguish for which she had no name.

"Kora!"

A Paniscus stood in her path. Phlebas. He was much the largest of the Panisci. He looked an old fifteen, his horns were long and crooked, and his haunches bristled with coarse red hairs.

"Where are you going?"

"To Centaur Town." She spoke curtly because his question was curt, though she rather pitied his hoof-loose, aimless life.

"Why not come to my house?"

"I'm out to barter this linen cloak for a mattock." Panisci neither bathed, nor trimmed their hair, nor washed their hooves. They looked as if they had wallowed in everything swept out of a house after a thorough housecleaning. She would have liked to give him a bath, but she knew that he would resist water as a fish resists the land. Poor little ragamuffin, she thought, ashamed of her original pique. With no adults to guide him, was it any wonder that he lived and looked as he did? It did not occur to her to be frightened of him. The Panisci had never bothered her in the past, except for Phlebas's suggestive remark about a grape which shrivels into a raisin.

He snatched at the cloak but she whipped it out of his grasp. He grinned at her. "I could barter it too. Give it to me."

She quickened her pace. She could easily defend herself against a single Paniscus. His horns were sharp, but in spite of her seeming fragility, she was agile enough to avoid them. Suppose, however, that he had brought his friends? He sauntered from the path but almost at once the bushes on either side of her began to crackle. A hoofbeat, the swish of a tail, a lewd snicker. She began to run. She had left the oaks of the Dryads, and among the cypresses, those funereal cones with their bronze-tinted leaves, there was no one to help her, not even a friendly Centaur.

She burst into a clearing. Thank Zeus she was out of the trees, usually her friends, but now a possible ambush. In the blaze of the morning sun, among the daisies and buttercups, what could harm her? Wolves skulked only in the dark and vampire bats moved like shadows among shadows. But regardless of sunlight and sunbright flowers, a band of Panisci—eight of them—emerged from the trees and, with smiling faces and slow, deliberate steps, surrounded her. Children, yes; but children in bands can be murderous. They joined hands and she found herself in a living prison.

"What do you want?" she cried, trying to keep the quaver out of her voice.

A snicker, a bleat; otherwise, silence. They began to circle her as if they were enacting some strange rite to the Lady Moon. Round and round they moved, swung, reeled, until she became quite dizzy from the sight of them.

"Is this what you want?" She flung the linen cloak to Phlebas.

"Yes," he said, snatching it out of the air and draping it around his hairy shoulders to cavort over the grass like a tipsy maenad.

Perhaps, she thought, I can make a break through the hole he has left in the chain.

"And this?" She tossed him her ring, an intaglio chiseled by the Telchins.

"Yes!" There was no chance for a break. Now they all loosed their hands, but only to snatch at her, slap at her, prod her with hairy fingers.

"What else, you dirty little boys?"

Phlebas threw back his head and his laughter was like the bleating of a dozen goats. He did not laugh like a child.

*   *   *   *

The Panisci were much too lazy to build their own houses. They used the tunnels and warrens and other constructions deserted by the giant beavers which had once lived in the country but which had been the first casualties in the War with the Wolves. And being thieves, the Panisci hid the tunnel mouths with bushes and stones to confuse their pursuers.

Phlebas's band occupied a lodge of mud and branches in the middle of a small lake originally dammed by the beavers. In the time of the beavers, the lodge had contained both a dry shelf and a covered pool, but the Panisci, disliking water, had filled the pool with mud and they reached the lodge by scrambling through a tunnel under the lake and then ascending sharply into a round, low room which appeared to be not so much decorated as littered. The original inhabitants, a blunt though circumspect race, would have been horrified to see the heaps of decaying leaves which took the place of beds, the moth-eaten wolfskin laid on a slab of wood which might, with a wrench of the imagination, be called a table, the crude earthen pots, half of them overturned in puddles of juice, the other half reeking with rancid milk or olive oil. The only attractive objects appeared to have been stolen. A gown which had come from the loom of a Dryad. A pruning fork which Chiron had missed last week from his vineyard. Gems from the workshop of a Telchin. And there—What was that shimmering tunic of unknown material which someone had carefully smoothed and hung on the wall? It was certainly not wool or linen.

As for the inhabitants, there must have been a dozen Panisci, no, thirteen, and there were four Bears of Artemis—shameful little hussies—who were keeping company with the Goat Boys. Since both Boys and Girls attained a physical development of from twelve to fifteen and since puberty comes to the Beasts at eleven or twelve, they sometimes formed unions which were rarely lasting—in fact, the Boys often shared a Girl in common—but which might produce offspring. Two of the four Girls were absentmindedly cradling infants: a cub and a kid.

The Girls were outcasts from their own race. They lacked

the fastidious charm of their more civilized sisters who lived in hollow logs and wove berry chains to make a decent living. Their paws were red and coarse, their fur was long and unkempt. The necklaces they wore were not of black-eyed Susans but strand upon garish strand of metal and other bright oddments stolen or dug from the earth or found in stream beds. They were a brazen lot, these Girls. They looked at Kora as if she had come to steal their men and it shocked her to see such knowing stares on such young faces. It was even rumored that they chewed the leaves of the hemp plants, which the Centaurs had imported from their travels in the East, and enjoyed exotic visions or fell into a drugged stupor. Indeed, one of the Girls was huddled in the corner, oblivious to her comrades and looking as if she were watching a private vision. Someone spoke to her but she neither moved nor changed her expression.

"Eirene's out of it," another Girl said.

"Well, she'll miss her supper."

"Do you think she cares? I've a mind to join her."

"The weed can wait. After the fun."

Kora, it seemed, was the fun. Phlebas flung her into their midst as a hunter might have flung a haunch of venison to his hungry comrades. The thought occurred to her that she might be intended for dinner. She knew that they preferred vegetables—grass, roots, the lower branches of trees, preferably vegetables stolen from the Centaur gardens—but that they ate almost anything, including leather sandals. Well, she thought, with that wry, self-depreciating humor which sometimes salted her dreams. Half of them will go hungry. There isn't enough of me for thirteen portions.

But they did not have her in mind for dinner. Not yet, at least. Having little to occupy them and being children or at least childish, they were curious creatures, and a Dryad in their lodge was an object of intense curiosity. They ogled her and poked her—she slapped their hands. They pinched her and prodded her—she kicked one of them in the shin and sent him limping across the room.

"Let's dunk her in the lake."

"Let's yank out that pretty hair by the roots."

"Let's cut her up and see how she tastes." (Now it was coming.)

The imagination of children is unlimited. She shuddered; the taste of fear was nightshade in her mouth. But her dignity did not forsake her. She drew herself to her full height of five feet so that she might tower above them in what she hoped was an awesome manner; she smoothed the linen gown which they had rumpled; she wriggled her foot and straightened her sandal.

"You are horrid children, all of you," she said. "And if you don't let me go, Eunostos and the Centaurs will drag this pitiful lodge right under the water. They can swim, you know, even if you can't."

"And drag you under with it? Besides, they don't even know you're here," said Phlebas.

The group reacted as if he had told a hilarious joke: the Boys stamped their hooves and the Girls clapped their paws. "They don't even know you're here!"

With that, they snatched the gown from her back so unexpectedly that she understood their success as thieves. And they vied with each other insulting the modest dimensions of her breasts. (Zoe should be in my place, she thought.)

Shivering in that ill-lit, ill-heated place, for there was no window to let in the sun—merely the fitful flickering of a fire on the clay floor and some beeswax candle stubs—she almost lost her courage. She sat on the floor by the fire and the thought of Eunostos (he would track her abductors) prevented her from breaking into tears or huddling like a frostnipped swallow to warm herself and hide her breasts.

A Paniscus kid, whose mother, she supposed, had forgotten

him in the midst of merriment, crawled into Kora's lap. She started to remove him and his stench of onion grass and sour milk. But he smiled up at her with a winsome innocence, his little horns peeping through his hair like toadstools. She took heart at the sight of this brave, pathetic child, whose mother appeared so indifferent to him.

What a dear little kid, she thought, to live in such surroundings. He raised his hand to the Centaur pendant which her captors had neglected to remove along with her gown.

"Do you think it's pretty?" she cooed. "You may play with it if you like."

Hardly had she finished her invitation than he bit her finger, snatched the pendant from its chain, and, scuttled to his mother with the booty.

"That's a good child," cooed the mother, in imitation of Kora.

Now Kora did begin to cry, though the wound to her pride was far greater than the pain from the bite. Green blood oozed from her bitten finger.

"What are you, some kind of vegetable?" Phlebas asked. "Look at that, boys, we have a lettuce among us."

"Did you think that everybody's blood was red?" she snapped. She was so angry now that she forgot to cry. "We live in trees and eat acorns. Why shouldn't our blood be green?"

"Suit yourself," said Phlebas. "But we'll stick to red. Won't we, boys?"

The Boys assented with a simultaneous bleat. The Girls, who had not been asked and whose blood was closer to brown than to red, remained silent.

Fortunately for Kora, the Panisci were soon distracted and they quite forgot the novelty of green blood and indeed of Kora. They returned to their usual pursuits—that is, horseplay and idleness. One of the Girls had donned Kora's robe and, while it was so large for her that it dragged the ground, at least it concealed her hairy flanks. She began to dance and stumble about the room, improvising a song—to Kora it was more like a howl—while Panisci stamped on the earth and set up a savage drumbeat, and Phlebas took a tortoiseshell lyre from a wall peg and accompanied the song with a monotonous plucking which sounded like nothing so much as a series of bat squeaks. But the sound suited the words:

> *"Bats and rats and spiders too,*
> *Out of the earth we conjure you:*
> *Wax the wings of the honey bee,*
> *Drag the Dryad down from her tree!"*

The weed-drugged Girl in the corner had roused herself sufficiently to struggle to her feet, and she was standing in one spot and swaying to the music as if it had merged with her vision. But not everyone was singing and dancing. There was never unanimity among the Panisci and their women, whatever their pursuits. Some had started to eat, with much smacking of lips and sucking of fingers, and a total disregard for the musicians. They seemed to make no distinction between a raw, unwashed root and a chunk of rancid fish, a grub or a toadstool. One of them tossed a tidbit to Kora, which she caught, examined, and discarded in disgust. A large white slug, lethargic but still alive.

"Why waste food on her?" pouted the mother of the thieving child. Phlebas cuffed her across the mouth. "Where's your mind, up in the trees? You know we can't afford to lose her. Remember the bargain." Two Panisci held her arms while a third, retrieving the slug, forced it into her mouth.

"Eunostos will find me," she gagged as the tail of the creature slithered down her throat.

"He's too big for the tunnel. He might wriggle in like a snake, but we would brain him before he got very far. As for the Centaurs, they couldn't get low enough to wriggle. And if they try to swim, we'll stand on the roof and hit them in the water with our slingshots."

"What do you mean to do with me?" Kora, at the very mention of Eunostos's name, had recovered her outward poise if not her inward composure, and she asked the question with quiet defiance.

"What do you think?" he leered, the dirty-minded little boy. The leer vanished when the Girl he had cuffed, apparently his woman, stamped on his hoof.

"Wait and see," he sulked to Kora.

She did not have long to wait.

The singing died to a hum, lips ceased to smack, a bone clattered to the floor. The rancid air smelled now of honey and pollen. Someone was approaching the lodge through the tunnel.

A queen of the Thriae stepped into the room and brushed the dirt from her gossamer wings. With a curt dip of a wing, she acknowledged and dismissed the entire gathering of Boys and Girls and walked immediately to Kora.

"My dear," she asked, drawing the girl to her feet, "what have they done to you? They've stolen your gown and they are smudges of dirt all over your face! Never mind, you're safe with me. My name is Saffron and we're going home."

"But how did you find me?" Kora sobbed. It was the same queen she had spied above Eunostos's trunk.

"When one has wings, one sees everything."

No one tried to stop her as she recovered her stolen robe and hastily slipped it over her shoulders, as she followed Saffron out of the ill-smelling chamber, and as she stepped into the welcome light of the declining sun. Behind her, most of the sounds did not resume. Someone sang a line of that revolting song, "Wax the wings of a honey bee," but the singer was interrupted by what sounded like a slap across the mouth, and Kora hoped that Saffron had not understood the words. It was clear that most of those disreputable children, though they had flouted all the other decencies, were awed by authentic royalty.

In the light and air, she swayed like a wind-shaken sapling; she thought at first that she was going to fall. But Saffron steadied her with a small jeweled hand.

"Just a little longer, my dear, and you shall rest and bathe and eat and be your beautiful self again." Saffron took her arm and guided her across the field.

"But my tree lies the other way."

"You're to be my guest."

"I'm deeply grateful to you, but right now I ought to go home. My mother will be sick with worry, and so will Eunostos."

"I shall send them word of your safety. Eunostos will no doubt come to fetch you." At the edge of the woods three sullen workers, as stiff and colorless as clay idols, awaited the return of their queen. At Saffron's command, they thundered into the air and converged on Kora with grasping hands.

"But I thought you rescued me!" she screamed as her feet left the ground.

"I bought you, my dear, and dearly. With a silken tunic and five silver anklets." (As a matter of fact, they were tin.)

CHAPTER IV

EUNOSTOS, on his way to visit Kora, had joined me in my tree for a mug of beer.

"Zoe, why are you sad?" he asked. "And why are you looking at me as if I made you sadder?"

"Not sad," I insisted. "Merely—thoughtful."

"No, sad. Are you worrying about the Thriae?"

How could I tell him that the Thriae were not in my thoughts (though perhaps they should have been)? That I was sad because he was growing up and I, who had loved him in two ways, first as a little calf, then as a daydreaming youngster, might come to love him in another, more hurtful way? Jolly Zoe, my lovers say of me. She loves us and leaves us with never a sign of regret. I try to preserve my image. Who wants a moody mistress (and I have no wish to be a wife)? But I do have my moods.

How could I tell him, too, that I foresaw a great deal of pain for one so kind and vulnerable, even in the kindly Country of the Beasts (for so it still seemed), and it would break my heart to see him hurt by Kora?

"I was thinking about when I was your age," I hedged. "I was as slim as a young sycamore and all the Centaurs, were in love with me. That was even before your father's time."

"The Centaurs still love you," he said. "Old and young. You're so maternal."

I fought down the urge to spank him and smiled as if he had paid me a princely compliment. "Thank you, my dear. But the hooves beat less frequently at my door."

"But you always tell me never to look back without a chuckle. Life's a jester, not a headsman. Isn't that what you say?

"You're right," I laughed. "I wouldn't change my life for all the pearls in the Great Eastern Sea."

"Neither would I," he said. "Your life, I mean. Now take your house. At Myrrha's house, I have to wipe my hooves on a mat before I go inside. But here everything is so—" He groped for a word. "Informal."

Yes, that was a tactful word. He might have said chaotic. My one-room house, lodged in a tangle of branches and reached, not like Kora's room by a ladder inside the trunk, but by an outside ladder of grapevines, had scarcely known a housecleaning. Half of its walls were windows, none of them with parchment, and I let the wind and the sun do most of my cleaning. My furnishings were few. A pile of wolfskins for a bed. A block of wood for a table. A round cupboard hewn from a stump and stocked with cheeses, loaves of bread, and a skin of beer. (You understand that when a Dryad uses wooden furniture, she makes sure that the wood has come from a tree which died from natural causes—lightning, drought, old age—and not from a live tree murdered by woodsmen.) A wardrobe consisting of a tunic and three ankle-length gowns, one of them in the Cretan style with open bodice to reveal my breasts (a gift from a Cretan lover). A single papyrus scroll, *The Indiscretions of a Dryad,* for light reading on the few evenings I spent without company (it is the only poem I understand, full of laughs and definitely not an epic—a gift from Eunostos). What more does a still-popular Dryad need to amuse herself and her men?

And there was always my tree for companionship, as shaggy and disheveled as an old dog, and just as beloved. We Dryads live with our trees and also we die with them, or die without them if for some reason we are separated for more than a few days. Should we die by accident while our tree still flourishes, then a blood relative takes our place, and many generations of Dryads have been known to inhabit the same durable oak. In my own case, the oak had belonged to my mother and grandmother before me and I reckoned its age to be a thousand or more, if indeed it was not as old as the pyramids.

"I have to go now," he said in a voice which implied: "But I could be coaxed into staying a little longer."

"Since when was Eunostos concerned with time?"

"It's the Thriae," he admitted.

"You think they might be up to some mischief?"

"You said yourself they were thieves. I saw one yesterday and didn't like the look of her. And Kora is so trusting."

"You're right, I did say they were thieves. But for all we know, they might have returned to the mainland."

"I hope so. Still, I just better make a door for Kora's house. A wolfskin isn't going to keep out thieves."

"That's her mother's concern. She can get a door from the Centaurs."

"She's a bit forgetful these days. Besides, she hasn't as much to trade as she used to."

"So you have to do her work."

"I haven't till now, unless she asked me. I'm not very dolent."

"You mean you're indolent?"

"That's what I said."

"But you've been busy with your poems."

"A Minotaur with gainly hoof," he began to recite. "I do think that one has possibilities. But"—and a wistful maturity shone in his young face—"poems don't build doors. I'm not even a traveling singer who can hawk his poems for bread. From a practical point of view, I must get on with my carpentry."

The Thriae had alarmed him more than I had anticipated. I almost wished that I had not told him about their inclinations.

"One more mug of beer and then you shall go."

The old Eunostos, the dreamy boy, reasserted himself and he dawdled over the beer.

"I've thought of a rhyme for 'mane,'" he said at last. "Lain."

"Eunostos, what is on your mind?"

"Well, it's better than 'bane,' and certainly 'slain' won't do. I don't want a sad ending. I want her to come into his arms, as it were. She left the bed wherein she lain..."

"Laid. Your mother would come back from the Underworld

if she knew an ignorant Dryad like me had to correct her son's grammar."

"I'm a poet, not a grammarian. But you're right. It's lie, lay, laid." With that he sprang to his hooves, kissed my cheek, and clambered down the ladder.

"Eunostos, come back soon."

"I will, Zoe."

"And next time, stay longer."

"I promise."

*   *   *   *

In the forest, he jumped and kicked his hooves together and tried to tell himself that he was as happy as he had been in the field of yellow gagea, composing his poem. Before the storm. Before the arrival of the Thriae. After all, he had just visited his best friend (his own word for me). But his hooves returned heavily to the earth, his head bowed, and the lines of the poem flew right out of his mind.

He sensed at once that there was something unnatural about Kora's house. In appearance it was unchanged, the same reed walls, the same red-ringed windows like square smiles. A trim, happy house which seemed a natural outgrowth of its tree. Then he realized that there was absolutely no sound even as he approached the door. Myrrha was not chattering to Kora, and she was not even humming at her preparations for supper. Had she gone to visit the Centaurs? Most unusual at suppertime, when she should have been frying pigeon eggs in a terra cotta skillet over the stone brazier.

Without waiting to knock, Eunostos lifted the wolf-skin and stepped into shadows, for the sun had already set and no lamp had been lit. Only the brazier, devoid of skillet or eggs, gave a thin, flickering light. Myrrha was lying on the couch, her body sunk in cushions and protected by a cloak of funereal black.

She turned her head and faced him, as white as a sun-bleached shell.

"Kora didn't come home."

"Where did she go?" The implication had not yet reached him.

"For a walk. But she didn't come home. And that was before breakfast."

Kora was known to be fond of solitary walks, but even when she ventured to the compound of the Centaurs, she never spent more than a morning away from her tree.

In a word, Kora was lost.

Eunostos felt as if he had plunged into a stream of melting snow. First he was numb; then the cold went through him like splinters of ice.

"Did you look for her?"

"Yes. And the Centaurs. All afternoon. All we found was a shred of cloth from her gown. And hoofmarks. Eunostos, I think the Panisci have her."

*   *   *   *

The news of Kora's disappearance reverberated through the forest. She had no enemies, so we thought, and we—her fellow Dryads, the Centaurs, even the little Bears of Artemis—were shamed and frightened by our failure to find her. Myrrha was inconsolable. Moschus brought her beer. The Bears of Artemis brought her pails of blackberries. I brought her a smoked goose and a loaf of bread. She greeted all of us with the same blank expression. She moved with a slow, shambling gait and spoke in monosyllables or disconnected phrases.

And what about Eunostos? She did not know where he had gone when he fled from her house; she hardly remembered his going. Others were a little more helpful. The evening of Kora's disappearance, a Bear Girl had seen him cross the meadow of yellow gagea.

"It was like there were bees after him," she said. "He didn't even speak to me. And he's usually so friendly." A Paniscus who, like most of his self-centered race, seemed unconcerned about Kora, thought that he remembered seeing Eunostos head for the hills which climbed toward Mt. Ida. On the other hand, he mused, it was dark and he might have seen a Centaur boy.

Needless to say, I went in search of him myself as soon as I had seen that Myrrha was in good hands. Misled by the Paniscus, I lost the whole morning in the foothills of Mt. Ida. But in the afternoon, I tracked his hoofprints to the limestone ridge which shuts most of our country from the outer world of the Cretans. There, in the darkest and most inaccessible cave, I found him huddled so tightly that you would have thought him a bear cub instead of a six-foot Minotaur. "Eunostos."

Silence. Then, as if from the end of a beaver's warren, the slow, reassuring words. "Yes, Aunt Zoe."

"But my dear, you've had an accident."

"It was the Panisci."

"But how did you get here?"

"I don't remember. I must have wandered here after they beat me up."

"Well, now you're coming home with me!"

*　　*　　*　　*

He had been roughhoused from hoof to tail—not exactly mauled, you understand, not quite crippled, but scratched, clawed, bitten, and butted in a fashion which indicated a pack of cowardly Panisci. It was all that I could do to push him up my ladder and guide him to a couch, where he sank to his haunches and dropped his head into his hands. I was barely able to keep him from toppling onto the floor.

"My poor calf," I cried, brushing the mane from his eyes and baring a large gash across his forehead. "What have they done to you?"

"I went looking for Kora. I thought the Panisci had her." He coughed and shuddered. "You know how they've lechered after her."

"And—?"

"They didn't have her, but Phlebas—he's the cross-eyed one—said he wished they did. He knew what to do with her even if I didn't. I rammed him in the belly until he admitted that they had had her but had sold her to one of the Bee queens. Then his friends jumped me. I could have handled three or four. But six at the same time! After that, I don't remember a thing till you found me in the cave."

"Wait till Chiron hears about this," I muttered angrily. "The Thriae will wish they had never blown this way. Have you any idea which queen?"

"Not really. But the one who spied on Kora and me was wearing a tiger-colored tunic. Will that help?"

"It may help a great deal. Each of them seems to have her special color. But no more talking now, Eunostos. You're no good to Kora like this." I managed to stretch his long frame onto the couch. His hooves stuck over the end, but I supported them with a stool. I bathed his face with a cloth dipped in rose water and raised his head on a pillow.

"Drink," I said, and he sipped a few drops of potion concocted from basil, tansy, and marjoram. "It will ease your pain." It was also a sedative; it would sooth him into a healing sleep.

His tail twitched less nervously and finally subsided into a gentle swish. His eyelids drooped. The last thing he said to me was, "I'm going after that queen." Then he fell asleep.

I knew, however, that no sooner had he regained his strength than he would go charging down my ladder and after the Thriae, who would hardly receive him with open wings. There was one solution. I would go to her hive ahead of him. Utilizing my feminine wiles, I would learn the truth about Kora. Why the queen had bought her from the Panisci. What I could do to release or rescue her without at the same time endangering her life. If I failed in my mission, I would hasten to Chiron and ask him to summon a conclave of Beasts for immediate action. Not only would he recover Kora, we would drive those devious Bee-Folk from our forest. Chiron was old and trusting and he had not confronted a real menace since the War with the Wolves in my own girlhood. Being a Centaur, he was especially trusting when it came to women. But he was also fair and he knew that I would not make false accusations.

I knelt beside the couch where Eunostos slept. "My dear, my dear," I whispered. I will find your girl for you. Trust your old Aunt Zoe."

CHAPTER V

I KNEW THAT there were six hives of Thriae in the forest, each in its own style, each with its own queen, workers, and drones. The Bears of Artemis, who miss little in spite of their shyness, directed me to the hive of Saffron, the queen with the tiger-striped tunic. A drone was leaning against a tree and grinning up at me in a bold and suggestive fashion. He looked as if he possessed the imagination but not the energy to be a rogue. He would rather violate twenty women in his mind than pursue one in the flesh.

"Dear girl, he said. "I see you've come bearing gifts. Acorns is it, and what's this, a baked partridge? How quaint. Are they for me? My name is Sunlord." There was almost a feminine coquetry in his tone.

Clad in a loincloth brief enough to embarrass even a Cretan, he was smooth and brown and soft, with gauzy wings banded in black and gold. His slanted eyes were as gold as the bands on his wings, and I recalled that the Thriae had originally come from the land of the slant-eyed Yellow Men. They had been expelled by the natives for thievery and kidnapping, but not, it would seem, until there had been some mingling of races. There was no question that he was handsome, but so are banded serpents and the tigers which the roving Centaurs have fought in the jungles of the remote East.

"They're for your queen," I said with some asperity. "I've come to welcome her to the Country of the Beasts. Will you show me to her?"

Languidly he lifted a hand bejeweled with opals and malachites and pointed over his shoulder. I noticed that he wore anklets of golden bells, which tinkled when he uncrossed his ankles.

"Straight ahead. You can't miss her. She's the one with the bosom."

Apparently enervated by our conversation, he settled back against the tree and pretended to close his eyes. Still, I saw that he was carefully watching me.

A pretty fellow, I thought, but in spite of his naughty looks as sexless as a tadpole. Kora would come to no harm from the likes of him; and the other drones who lounged among the trees or nestled in the grass looked no less depraved but no more energetic. A Babylonian king who wished to people his court with eunuchs would find them ready-made in these soft males. I understood why the queen in her nuptial flight must be accompanied by a number of drones; in all of that number, she was lucky to find a single male to pleasure, much less fecundate, her.

And then I saw the hive. Built in the shape of a hexagon, it was too large for a house, too small for a palace, and seemingly too vulnerable for a fort. Its framework was of slender tree trunks. The workers had obviously uprooted the trees with utter ruthlessness and I was only relieved to find that they had utilized willows instead of oaks. Now they were facing the trunks with clay, and, where the clay had dried, glazing it with a material which resembled wax. Some of the workers were wheeling out of the sky with deep-bottomed bowls of clay from the banks of the Beaver Lake. Others were producing the wax. The production was not a pleasant process. Three workers were wading, waist deep, in a vat like an oversized wine press and, with the help of ladles, mixing a base of resin with an excretion from their own bodies, an odorless, colorless liquid which poured from their undersized breasts, or nipples I should say, since their breasts were no more than an intimation. (To a worshipper of the Great Mother like myself, it seemed unspeakable that a bosom should be perverted to such a use. Poor things, I suppose it was the only kind of maternity they knew, giving birth to building materials.) Once the resin and waxy excretion were properly mixed, other workers arrived to trowel it onto the hardening clay of the walls, where in turn it hardened into a glistening, yellowish glaze no less decorative than the thin sheets of alabaster with which the Cretans face their palaces. When the edifice was finished, it would dazzle the eye like a huge, many-faceted topaz.

Having first observed the workmanship, I now more closely observed the workers and confirmed my first impression that they were the least feminine females I had ever met. They were gray, hairy, and thick-bodied, with stubby wings which looked insufficient to lift them from the ground. The wings beat incessantly and thunderously, and the workers managed to fly out of sheer mindless exertion. All of them wore a single expression, or lack of expression, bordering on petulance (and none of them wore any clothes). Their queen was flitting among them and giving stern and precise orders in a voice of incongruous sweetness. "Apply wax here." "Let the clay dry there." "Who fetched this rotten timber? I told you precisely which trunks to cut." She was as beautiful as a phoenix even when she frowned, and she did nothing but frown until she saw me.

Then she smiled and never once, during all the time that I talked to her, did she relax that fixed and perfect smile. Identified by her tunic of tiger-striped silk, she was small and delicate, with feet about the size of my big toe. Her wings were as tenuous and brilliant as a dew-touched spider web in a burst of sunlight. Her eyes, like those of the drones, were slanted so that they seemed somehow not to share in the smile even when her lips curved upwards and her small white teeth glittered with pearled perfection. But an alien goddess and not our own Great Mother had fashioned her. She lacked amplitude, and I do not mean of proportion. I mean of spirit. What was littleness in her body was pettiness in her soul.

"My dear neighbor," she said, casually stroking what appeared to be a foxtail draped around her neck. "Your coming is as the new moon out of the frosty treetops. I wish that I had tiger lilies to strew at your feet. I wish that I had myrrh to bathe your ankles..."

I am a blunt woman myself and her niceties began to cloy. I shoved forward my basket. "I'm Zoe, the Dryad, and I've brought you some acorns and a partridge."

"Acorns and a partridge," she echoed, with seeming delight (and perhaps a tinge of mockery for the graceless rustic who brought such inelegant gifts?). "A rarity of rarities." The foxtail twitched; it was obviously alive and did not belong to a fox.

I fought down the urge to throw the partridge in her face and break her porcelain composure. I must not jeopardize my mission with any outbursts of temper; I must imitate Kora.

"I have come to welcome you to the Country of the Beasts."

"Your presence in itself is a welcome. Your gifts are beyond measure." What would she have said if I had brought her diamonds or sapphires? "As you see, my humble dwelling is far from finished. Still, there is a room where we may visit and exchange those confidences which unite the ladies of all lands. Perhaps you will teach me the customs of your land so that I may comport myself with fitting decorum. In my own country, I was a queen. Here, I am a guest, and perhaps I may unintentionally give offense."

The so-called humble dwelling was a labyrinth which would have put the famous architect Daedalus to shame. The wax-glazed walls glittered like many mirrors, and at every turn we confronted our own images: Saffron's perpetual smile, my own stout, reddish features which looked unbelievably coarse beside such exquisiteness and which, try as I might, wore a look of stoic determination instead of pleased expectation. Corridors led into corridors, rooms into rooms. Candelabra, burning with myriad lily-shaped candles, hung from the ceilings and bathed us in a shifting gauze of light. In one room, honey bees were depositing nectar in silver bowls; in another, a worker with a ladle was mixing pollen and wine and stirring the mixture as vigorously as a female Centaur might sweep a floor. Finally we found ourselves in Saffron's audience room, hexagonal like the hive and apparently situated at its exact center.

Leopard skins covered the floor to a thickness of several inches, and the black and golden spots, reflected endlessly in the polished walls, gave me the feeling of a jungle infested with beautiful, merciless animals. A wicker chair, supported by silken threads and backless to accommodate the wings of the queen, swayed from the ceiling. In the center of the room there was a stone pedestal curiously lacking a statue. Perhaps it was intended to hold an image, as yet uncarved or uncast, of a winged deity.

She shrugged a tiny helpless shrug. "Because of the storm, we arrived with few belongings. You must forgive my poor room. Not even a statue for my pedestal." (Never mind, I thought. Given a little time and you'll have stolen all you need.) She motioned me to the skins and nodded deprecatingly at the chair. "You will not find it comfortable." (She meant that my weight would snap the supporting threads.) With a brief flutter she settled into a chair, dangling her ankles, and peered down at me with a curious mixture of deference and—derision? Defiance? I could not read such inscrutability. I took my revenge by imagining her a cockatoo on a perch in the palace of an Egyptian pharaoh, and the ludicrous image salved my pride.

"And the Minotaur youth. Your noble-maned young friend? I saw him with you the day of our arrival. Where is he now?"

"His name is Eunostos and he got in a fight when he—"

"Yes?"

I might as well tell her the truth and watch her reaction. "When he quarreled over a Dryad with a band of Panisci. He thought they had kidnapped her."

"And had they?" She never flickered an amber eyelash.

"Yes. But they sold her, it seems. Nobody knows who bought her."

"A pity. But this Eunostos. I should imagine he gave a good account of himself."

"He always does," I said proudly. "This time he took on six at once and left all of them with a cracked horn or a broken hoof. He's recovering in my tree."

"I trust his injuries will heal? Nothing vital is permanently impaired?"

"Nothing at all."

"A beastly young bull," she said with admiration, using the term "beastly" as we do here in the country, just as a Man might say "manly." Saffron herself was a Beast according to our definition, much as I hated to claim her.

Then I saw the pendant; Kora's pendant, the silver effigy of her Centaur father. Or rather I caught a tiny glimpse of silver horns glinting in an open casket of jewels: anklets of amber from the rivers of the far north, ivory necklaces from the land of the Nubians, malachite pins from the local workshop of the Telchins and no doubt stolen from them. It may have been foolish or forgetful of her to entertain me in the very room which contained incriminating evidence. Perhaps my visit had taken her by surprise. On the other hand, the queens of the Thriae are supremely confident that their smooth tongues can extricate them from any predicament. Precautions seem to them beneath their pride.

I tried to look inscrutable and, so far as I could tell from her frozen smile, she had not observed my discovery.

"Well," I said, "I have kept you from your workers long enough." I could not resist adding, "They seem to need some direction."

She laughed. "Indeed. They have two virtues, strong wings and mindless obedience."

"And the drones?"

"One virtue at best. But we must make do with the resources at hand, mustn't we?" Her interest in Eunostos was becoming clear. If the resources at hand were typified by Sunlord, why not be resourceful and search at a distance?

"I trust you will be happy here in the Country of the Beasts," I said with as much grace as I could summon, though my voice resounded through the rooms and corridors like the afterecho of an earthquake. "Next time you must come to see me." (Yes, and I will feed you hensbane.) "Follow the path between the cypresses, turn at the rock which looks like a Cretan galley, cross the meadow of yellow gagea, and there is my tree. You'll know it by its outside ladder and its abundant foliage."

"First you must accept a small token of my gratitude for your visit."

I waved a protesting hand—a few more amenities would suffocate me—but Saffron clapped her feet, her anklets jangled, and a worker appeared in the door.

"Bring my guest some refreshment."

In the time it takes to raise and lower a door hanging the worker reappeared with a goblet of amber wine.

"It's made from honey and fermented pollen," Saffron said.

"I never drink before lunch," I said firmly. Amenities or not, I had no intention of letting her poison me.

She looked surprised; her smile faltered but did not quite forsake her. "Then you must accept a small gift or I shall be deeply wounded." She reached to the back of her neck and drew down what, on closer examination, I saw to be a bird or animal. Owl? Rabbit? No, kind of a diminutive combination, bunnylike, feathery winged, which she cuddled in her hands.

"He's called a Strige. He's no trouble at all. Feed him sunflower seeds and he's quite content. Most of the time he sleeps, and what he likes most is to drape himself around your neck. He'll keep you as snug as a fox's tall and you won't have to bother with carrying him."

She draped him around the back of my neck. His warmth and softness were indescribable. I could feel and hear his soft purring and I must admit that I was enchanted with him. I will take him to Eunostos, I thought. He loves small animals and it will help to cheer him until we can rescue Kora. Besides, if I refuse to accept she may suspect that I have seen the pendant.

"But Saffron, all I brought you was acorns and a partridge, and you've given me your own pet!"

"The measure of a gift lies in the heart, and you have kindled a warm hearthfire in me with your friendship."

She waved to me as I left the encampment, and soon she was busily whisking among the workers and piping orders in her melodious but incontestable voice. The drones grinned their wicked, languorous grins and Sunlord said:

"I see you impressed our queen to the extent of her favorite Strige. Good for you, my girl."

I could not resist a parting sally. "Did you ever do a day's work, my boy?"

Unaccountably my voice lacked its usual resonance. No doubt I had lost my boom in the company of soft-spoken Saffron. Sunlord craned his neck to catch at my words and I had to repeat the insult. He took it with wry good grace.

"If I had, you wouldn't see me now, would you?"

As I strode into the forest, my first feeling was triumph. I had accomplished my purpose. I had proved Saffron's guilt. Now I would wake Eunostos and tell him what I had learned. If I found him sufficiently rested, we would call on the Centaurs and plan Kora's rescue. Why then did I feel a curious malaise? Why had my parting sally at Sunlord emerged as a whisper instead of a thunderous insult?

"Ho there, Moschus," I called to test my voice, though unhappily Moschus was not in sight. Even if he had been behind the next tree, he would not have heard my thin whisper. Now I was feeling downright somnolent. I'll stop a moment, I thought, and catch my breath. My adventure—the danger, the confrontation with a deceitful woman—has exhausted me. I leaned against the friendly bulk of a cypress trunk. I slid onto the ground and fought to open my eyes. Had Saffron drugged me? I had been so careful not to drink her wine!

The little creature around my neck had grown as heavy as a bronze collar. I tried to raise my arm to remove him. The arm fell to my side.

"Sleep well, my dear." My last image was Saffron standing over me, flanked by workers. Their thick hands were reaching toward me like knotty clubs.

"No," I gasped.

"Yes," she smiled. And I lost consciousness.

*   *   *   *

I came to my senses in a room whose walls were glazed with wax and whose sole furnishings consisted of two leopard-skin rugs, one of them under my prone, aching body, one of them under Kora.

"Kora!"

At least my voice had returned.

She stirred fitfully but she did not open her eyes. She was deathly pale; her green-gold hair lay in wild confusion about her face; her lips had turned blue. I knew the signs. She was not drugged, she was suffering the prolonged separation from her tree. The vital forces were slowly draining out of her.

Saffron, flanked by two workers, stood in the door. "How long does your friend have?" she asked.

"Without her tree, you mean? Five or six days. Seven at most. She'll weaken each day."

"And so will you, I presume. We've had her for three days and she's already peaked. I imagine you'll hold up better—because of your, how shall I say, bovinity."

"If you mean I'm fat, why don't you say so?" I snapped. "My lovers call me voluptuous, but you wouldn't know about that with your skinny little frame." I tried to struggle to my feet but sank back onto the skin. "Why don't you let Kora go? You have her pendant."

"Aren't you interested in how I captured you?"

"You must have drugged me. I don't know how, since I didn't drink your wine."

"No, and I had to lend you one of my friends."

I was slow to grasp her meaning. "The Strige?"

"Exactly. He relieved you of some excess blood. You see, his tongue is like a delicate needle. He inserted it into your neck without your feeling a thing and drew forth just enough blood to make you faint. Fortunately for you, we removed him before he had drunk his fill."

"Why doesn't he drink your blood?"

"It's yellow. He only likes green or red. You see, he's very particular, the dear little fellow."

I was quick with questions. "And Kora. Why did you buy her from the Panisci?"

"They captured her for me in the first place. For a price, of course."

"But why?"

"Bait."

"For Eunostos!" I shuddered. "You had her captured to bait him into your hive."

"Exactly. I entered into negotiations with a Paniscus chief— Phlebas, is he called? But he refused to deliver Eunostos without maiming him. Said it was quite impossible. He suggested that Kora would be easier handling and accomplish the same purpose."

"But what do you want with a harmless Minotaur calf?" As if I needed to ask!

"A young bull, I would say. Have you noticed his horns? The

best drone is barely adequate as a lover. Consider the one you met, Sunlord. Would he satisfy you?"

"I would rather remain a virgin than give him a try."

"Exactly. However, if a Dryad can mate with a Minotaur, why not a Thria? A full-grown Minotaur, to be sure, would be a trifle large for me. At the very least, he would muss my wings. But Eunostos is only six feet. It will be interesting to see what offspring he sires. Something more animated than a worker and more manly than a drone, I trust. Perhaps a winged bull like those you see in Hittite monuments."

"But isn't it true that the drone who mates with a queen is"—and my voice fell to a quaver—"doomed?"

"Our mating is somewhat turbulent. The drone is generally—and forgive my coarseness, but then I can't shock you, can I?—gutted."

CHAPTER VI

I HAD PARTIALLY recovered from my loss of blood to the Strige and not yet begun to feel the effects of separation from my tree. Thus, I was still alert if not exactly vigorous. But Kora, poor thing, was fading like a plucked chrysanthemum. Marmoreal whiteness had become unhealthy pallor, and the solar twinklings had departed from her hair. Her movements were slow, lethargic, labored. She needed immediate sustenance.

The waxen walls thudded dully but failed to crack when I smote them with my fist. The wooden door, bolted from the outside, creaked but did not yield beneath the weight of my shoulder. Our hastily constructed room was a constricting prison. Well, then, they must come to us. I stamped on the earthen floor and let out the roar of a wounded she-bear. Almost at once the flutter of wings announced the approach of visitors. Saffron, flanked by two gray workers, glared at me from the doorway. With my somewhat whimsical fancy, I pictured her as honey poured between slices of wheaten bread and imagined the three of them being devoured by a Cyclops.

"Are you trying to bring down the walls with your bellowing, you old cow?"

"I'm a Dryad, not a female Minotaur. There's no such thing. My friend is hungry and so am I." The workers were armed with bamboo spears, like giant stingers, narrowed to lethal points.

"Honey and pollen tea? Sorry, my dear, the offer is withdrawn. Or perhaps the partridge you brought me? It would hardly be gracious for a guest to eat her own gift. Besides, I've eaten it myself, and it was quite palatable. That's more than I can say for the acorns. I almost broke a tooth on the first one I bit."

"If there are any left," Kora began.

I hastened to interrupt her. If Saffron suspected that we

craved acorns, she would feed them to the squirrels. "I expect they were a little stale. Honey then? Pollen bread?" I pleaded.

"Food is in short supply while my workers are building the hive. Why should I waste it on temporary guests?"

"If we die too soon, you won't be able to show us to Eunostos and have your way with him."

"My beauty and my wiles should suffice."

"Not if he thinks you've killed us."

"I'll simply tell him you're my captives. I don't have to say whether you're dead or alive."

"He's been on his own for a year and he isn't easily fooled. You'd better keep us handy in case you need some proof."

She managed to scowl without wrinkling her flawless forehead. Her mouth curved down like an overturned bowl.

"Oh, very well, I guess I can spare you something." The bowl righted itself. "I'll send you a special dinner before I call on your friend."

Special dinner. Perhaps she intended to poison us.

"Never mind," I said to Kora when Saffron had left the room. "Eunostos will come looking for us. Did you know he's been scouring the forest ever since you disappeared? He got himself beaten up on your account."

"Is he badly hurt?" she cried.

"No, just a bit sore. He's recuperating in my tree."

"I'm not worthy of him. He thinks of me as a heroine out of his favorite epic, *Hoofbeats in Babylon*. People interpret my silence however they like. To Eunostos, it means mystery and wisdom."

"You may not be worthy of him, Kora." I was her best friend but also her frankest critic. "But you're worthier than most. He'll find us, you know, and when he does, see that you show your appreciation."

"Will he, Zoe?" Her voice lacked conviction. "I would give my Centaur pendant—if I still had it—to see him now."

"You never encouraged him much when you had the chance."

"Not in the way you mean. He seemed like a younger brother. Always stumbling over his hooves." I did not tell her that in some ways both of them were still children and that she, from her seemingly sublime eminence of eighteen years, was likely to stumble over her dreams. That is, if she lived to continue dreaming them.

Speech was beginning to tire her but silence was frightening to both of us. If any sounds came to our ears, it was the faint whirring of wings or the mellifluous piping of Saffron as she directed the workers. Finally the piping stopped. She's gone to my tree, I thought.

Then the workers brought us the promised dinner.

Saffron had sent us the uneaten acorns.

*   *   *   *

Eunostos opened his eyes and stared at the thatched roof above his head. He saw the walls which I had hung with tapestries commemorating my lovers, the square windows which filtered the light through a lattice of foliage. He smelled the bark and leaves of my tree. Zoe's house, he thought. But how did I come here? At last he remembered.

"Zoe."

"No. Saffron."

He recognized the queen who had spied on him in his garden. "How did you find this house?" he asked angrily.

"Zoe herself gave me directions. And she left the door unlatched. Of course I don't need ladders, though there was one handy if I did."

He was not in the least impressed with her fabled beauty. Yes, she was prettily formed, like a cowslip or a buttercup. Yes, her skin was as smooth and golden as honey, and her wings were a tremulous translucence as she stood above his couch and smiled down at him with what seemed to be admiration and expectation. But she doesn't have Kora's height, he told himself, nor Zoe's opulence, and there are too many bracelets on her arms, and her wings look as if the faintest breeze would shred them. Actually, he was not prepared to see anything good in a woman who might be responsible for Kora's disappearance.

"Don't look so angry!" she teased. "You look as if you would like to butt me. Did I wake you up, dear boy?"

"Yes, you did."

"Never mind. You'll sleep like a drone after we've had our little visit."

She sat down beside him on the couch, touching his leg with her thigh. The thigh felt silken beneath its thin silk tunic. He tried to contract himself away from her touch, but he was already pressing into the reeds of the walls. Perhaps resignation was indicated under the circumstances.

"You have a lot of hair on your chest to be so young," she remarked. "It's rather becoming, you know. Our drones never grow hair except on their heads. The only thing you can say for them is that they never get bald."

"We're born hairy. It keeps us warm in the winter. We don't get bald either. What do you want?"

"To visit, as I said. To talk. To become acquainted with the last Minotaur. But I shouldn't imagine you'll always be the last. You'll have sons and grandsons, and one day there will be a whole new tribe of Minotaurs. That is, if you choose the proper mate. One whose fertility matches your virility."

"Zoe isn't here now."

"You're not listening. I didn't come to see Zoe, I came to see you."

"I'm trying to listen. But you're sitting on my hoof. And how did you know I was here?"

"From Zoe. And Kora."

"Then you must be holding them prisoners!" Angrily he swung his arm and knocked her onto the floor.

She resumed her place on the couch as if she had fallen by accident. Her rueful laugh was like bells with copper tongues, sweet but metallic. Kora had laughed like wind chimes. "I see that no amenities are necessary between us, my dear. Yes, I am holding your two friends in my hive—unwilling guests, you could say—and it lies in your power to rescue them."

He glared at her. "What do I have to do?"

"Eunostos, I must tell you a sad truth. My daughters are diligent workers, but unintelligent and unresourceful. It has taken them seven days to build the hive, which is not yet finished. I myself have given them a long, proud lineage. I can trace my ancestry back to the days when the Yellow Men were living in crude stone huts and Cretans were cowering in caves. But the males of my tribe—well, to call them Beasts is a monumental exaggeration. The very best of them—Sunlord, for example— is a poor specimen of bestiality. At the next nuptial flight, I'm not even sure that I shall be able to conceive, and a queen who doesn't conceive is dethroned."

"In other words, you need a husband from another race."

"Precisely."

"Well, you might consider a Centaur."

She shuddered. "Too large. Too many legs."

"A Paniscus? They're the right size for you."

"Odorous. Onion grass, don't you know."

"Just who did you have in mind?"

Impatience flickered behind her smile. "Don't be dense, dear boy."

"Me?"

"Who else?"

"For a stud," he muttered. "Like the Cretan bulls who are bred for the ring."

"Stud? Husband, you mean. Didn't I speak of a nuptial flight? Or lover, if the notion of matrimony frightens you. Yes, Eunostos, you are to sire my next eggs. I spied you from the air when I first arrived in this land, and you seemed to me as a dragonfly to a rose. As a tiger moth to a night-blooming cereus. As a—"

"And that's *all* I have to do to rescue Kora and Zoe?"

"That's all," she snapped. The Thriae do not like to be interrupted in their figures of speech. "I have no other reason to hold them."

"Set them free first."

She pouted and turned her back. "You make it sound like a crude bargain. Here I've swallowed my pride and come to your arms like a common little Dryad, and you want guarantees of my good faith."

"At least give me proof you're holding them."

She proudly produced the Centaur pendant. "I believe this horsy fellow is a close relative of your dear one."

He nodded with reluctant recognition. "Kora's pendant. You do have them, then." He did not think to ask for guarantees of our safety. It never occurred to him that Saffron might have murdered or be in the process of murdering us. His bluff male heart could not conceive of such perfidy in a female.

"After all, what have you to lose?"

After all, what did he have to lose? He did not know the traditional fate of a drone.

"Am I so unlovely?" she continued. "Are my wings uncouth, my color disagreeable? Is this any way to treat a stranger in your land?"

"You're a bit skinny," he said, "and you must be a hundred or so."

"If you think me plain, you ought to see my workers. Why they don't even know how to paint their faces!"

"You've never taught them?"

"It might distract them from their work. As for my age, I am a hundred exactly without a so. This Zoe creature, I believe, is in her three hundreds."

"You've held up well at that," he admitted. "You're sure I won't tear your wings?"

"As sure as I am that the earth is flat and supported on the back of a giant tortoise."

At least she knew her science.

* * * *

With her small but insistent hand, she pushed him onto his back. Dear Zeus, he thought. After my bout with the Panisci, am I equal to pleasuring a Bee queen? He took a deep breath and flexed his muscles. He lashed his tail—the part which was not under him—until it cracked like a whip. He felt a touch of soreness in his flanks but otherwise Zoe's remedy and a restful sleep had worked a miracle. He ought to prove adequate, perhaps competent, possibly proficient. True, he had promised to wait for Kora at least a year. But it was for her sake that he was making his sacrifice. Surely she would understand, approve and appreciate.

Saffron sat beside him and, holding both of his horns, stared into his eyes. Then, with a hand no larger than a maple leaf, she rumpled his mane.

"Never trim it, my boy. It becomes you too well. And such large, lovely ears! They're translucent in this light. Like mother-of-pearl." For Kora's sake no sacrifice was too great. If necessary, he decided, he could endure further sacrifices.

First she was lying beside him. Then she was in his arms. Then her little tongue was flickering over his lips and her hands were teasing the hair on his chest into curls. There was something, after all, to be said for a skinny woman.

She had invited; now it was time to accept the invitation. When a lady opens the door and offers the hospitality of a warm hearth, does a man stand shivering in the snow? He entered the house with alacrity and, being a gracious guest, not without gifts...

Smiling, she took the gifts and, still smiling, she bit his ear. He slapped a hand to the bite and felt the dampness of blood. A love nip, he supposed. But why had her teeth met with quite such determined force?

She kicked him. A love kick? Hardly. He must have angered her. Perhaps she felt that he had treated her frail little body like that of a buxom Dryad. Perhaps, accustomed to her drones and in spite of what she said about them, she had wanted mincing caresses instead of stalwart embraces. His experience with women did not extend to Bee queens.

"Saffron," he started to apologize. "I'm used to the Dryads. If you'll just tell me how—"

She spat in his face. She became a hybrid of hybrids—griffin, hydra, chimera—and her body entwined him like a python, her arms constricted like tentacles, her thighs resembled a snapping sea turtle. Together they tumbled off the couch and momentarily his big frame was airborne as Saffron fluttered her wings with a frenzy of passion or anger or whatever possessed her.

That's it, he thought. She wants a nuptial flight! But I'm just not equipped to satisfy her.

That wasn't it, either. With her fourth kick he lost his patience. Eunostos had known passionate women in the four years since he had come of age, but Saffron's passion appeared to be born of fury instead of ardor: a venomous, vitriolic contempt for drones, Minotaurs, Men—males in general. He could not fathom her subtleties; he did not philosophize about the female who demands ascendancy, the goddess who requires the sacrifice of the god, the spider who devours her mate.

He simply fought her with his impaired but still prodigious strength. He was not a soft-bellied drone and he was not to be used or misused. She had bitten his ear; he bit her arm with teeth which a beaver might have envied. She kicked; he butted with horns whose heaviness gave them the force of small battering rams. She squeezed; he caught her neck between his hands and she fluttered like a chicken doomed to the pot.

In the end, the captive guest captured the house by storm.

Indignant but not in the least gutted, panting but not winded, a few scratches and bruises added to those sustained from the Panisci, he flung her onto the floor and sat on the couch to glower down at her frazzled body.

"And you call that lovemaking? What do you do when you hate a fellow?"

Her wings were frayed. Her tiger-striped tunic lay in shreds at her feet; the impeccable queen of the Thriae looked like a wench after a street brawl.

She stared at him with a stupefaction which rapidly became rage. "You weren't fair. You resisted me!"

"What was I supposed to do? Lie down and be bitten into chunks?"

"I'm a queen, you lout. You were supposed to die in my arms. It's expected."

"I'm only a carpenter but I have my principles."

With regal pride and obvious pain, she regained her footing and swayed toward the door.

Eunostos kept his seat and eyed her warily in case of further mischief. "And you're going to set Kora and Zoe free?"

"Of course not," she shrilled as she stepped out of the door and, nursing her wounded wings, fluttered toward the ground.

He stamped his hoof. Very well, then, he would have to rescue them.

"Partridge, Bion, we're going to war!"

CHAPTER VII

PARTRIDGE and Bion, as usual, were within an easy bellow of their friend Eunostos. They were in fact at the foot of Zoe's tree.

"We saw that Bee woman slither in the door," admitted Partridge, "and she seemed to be up to mischief. But I didn't want to interrupt till you called. You might have been trysting."

"You know I'm promised to Kora," snorted Eunostos.

"Well, you can't wait forever," said Partridge tolerantly, as he viewed the ravaged couch.

"As a matter of fact, we're going to rescue Kora now."

"Oh," said Partridge, who looked as if he would rather be grazing among the buttercups. But the more martial Bion waved his feelers and bared a pair of small but incisive teeth. In the secrecy of Kora's tree, hidden from Thriae scouts, if there were such, and treacherous Panisci, for there were certainly such, they formulated their plans. Eunostos was young but he was not so inexperienced as to think that he and his two friends (valiant though they were—well, Bion anyway) could charge the hive of a Bee queen and singlehandedly effect the rescue of Kora and me. He had read about such adventures: the stalwart Minotaur of *Hoofbeats in Babylon* had rescued a Babylonian princess from captivity among nefarious batmen by assaulting their cave at night and panicking them with his bellows. But that was an epic and Eunostos knew himself to be slightly too young for an epical hero, even though an epical heroine awaited his rescue.

He could even ask Chiron to attack the Thriae with a troop of Centaurs. Though the Centaurs could probably level the hive, in spite of the winged defenders with their bamboo spears, Kora and I might die in the carnage. Eunostos had witnessed Saffron at her most murderous and he no longer doubted that she would murder her hostages rather than allow them to be rescued. No, he must devise a stratagem. He must rely on subterfuge. He must somehow divert Saffron, the workers, and the drones so that he could enter the hive and rescue us, and only then unloose the Centaurs to launch an attack and forestall pursuit. Subversion must precede invasion.

"Hello up there!" came a cry from the foot of the tree. It was Moschus, the Centaur. "Has my girl forsaken me?"

Eunostos thrust his head out of the door and Moschus scowled.

"I guess she has. These days, the world belongs to the young."

"You don't understand," Eunostos said, clambering down the ladder, followed by Bion, and then a fat, puffing Partridge. And he explained the plight of both Kora and Zoe. Moschus, whose breath as usual smelled of beer, cried for an immediate assault on the hive. He whinnied and reared back on his hind legs, but Eunostos emphasized the need for caution.

"If you could just bring some of your friends to the woods nearby...you understand, they mustn't look warlike. They must look as if they've come to graze among the buttercups. And Partridge, why don't you go with Moschus?" Partridge must be made to feel useful without endangering himself and everyone else with his military ineptitude.

Partridge beamed with pride; he had been designated as an important messenger but not required to fight. Moschus was less pleased at having to take orders from a stripling of fifteen, and being equated, as it were, with an overweight Goat Boy.

"Partridge," he sulked, "must you eat onion grass?"

Together they departed among the oaks, the Centaur in the lead with the Goat Boy wheezing behind him.

"And Bion..." Bion's task was all-important. Eunostos spoke slowly and with simple words to make sure he was understood. Bion dipped his antennae in response and scurried off to his friends and their workshop.

*　　*　　*　　*

In less than an hour Eunostos had occupied a hollow tree with a peephole at the edge of the clearing where Saffron's workers were completing her hive. He was sure that they had not observed his approach. The were much too preoccupied with their work, and Saffron's insistence on a quick completion had apparently led them to neglect posting a scout in the air. Now, he must wait, must force himself to wait; a difficult task indeed for a young Minotaur whose lady is in the hands of an unprincipled Bee queen. He conjured her in his mind, an image of jade and alabaster mellowed by love. "My gallant Eunostos," he heard her cry. "Only you can rescue me from my enemies. Restore me to my tree and its healing walls of bark. Receive your just reward!" And Zoe, his dear Aunt Zoe, who had been like a mother to him.

Antennae waved in front of his eye. Bion stood on four legs outside the tree, his other four legs, with their hooklike feet, clutching the trunk and raising his round head to the level of Eunostos's peephole.

"Everything accomplished, Bion? And you brought some of your friends to help you?"

A flurry of feelers.

"Go to it, man!" He felt an onrush of love for this more-than-a-pet, this devoted companion. (Only for Kora and me would he risk the life of his friend.)

Bion emerged from the shrubbery and, at a leisurely pace for a Telchin, sidled among the workers as they mixed their wax and applied the finishing touches to the walls of their new hive. They were so intent on their work—for they had to work with haste, since the wax dried rapidly once it was dipped from the vat and applied to the walls—that they did not see him at first. Then one of them dropped her trowel and gave a buzz of pleasure, the first such emotion which Eunostos had ever seen in a worker. His assumption had been correct. The insect Beasts of the air would feel an immediate affinity, even if a certain condescension, for the insect Beasts of the earth. For one thing, they observed the same mating practices, the same nuptial flight of the queen and her potential lovers.

Bion approached the worker who had first spied him and, like a cat with an Egyptian, presented his back to be stroked. His body vibrated with feigned but convincing pleasure as her coarse fingers moved over his metallic skin and came to rest on his head.

"Girls," she cried. "We've found a pet." A log fell to the ground. Bodies no longer swished in the vat of wax. The ghost of a smile flickered into several of the faces, and the others lost their petulance.

"And I think he's brought us a gift."

Bion reached in the pouch which he wore around his neck and removed a bronze mirror in the shape of a swan. The worker accepted the mirror from his two forelegs and looked at the back, which was figured with winged dove goddesses who might almost have been Thriae, though all of them were beautiful enough to be queens. Obviously the poor worker was not familiar with the function of a mirror; she took it for a useless bauble, and beauty without practicality had, in the past, meant little to her. But turning the object in her hands, she saw the polished surface on the other side and caught her own reflection. Though she had looked at her sisters for years, she had clearly not imagined that she herself was quite so dour and sexless and altogether repugnant. She flung her hands to her face. One of her sisters retrieved the mirror, which had fallen to the ground, and discarded it with similar revulsion. It was not long before all twenty workers had seen themselves framed and branded as unbeautiful in this appalling gift.

At first it appeared that Bion would have to flee for his life. But Eunostos had anticipated just such a poisonous reaction and counseled Bion to arm himself with the antidote. The Telchin withdrew a vial of carmine from his pouch, flicked off the lid, dipped an antenna to the red cosmetic cream, and rubbed a generous portion onto the gray, leathery face of the worker nearest to him. She stood stonily while he made the application; she seemed to be deciding whether to hit him or give him a chance to redeem his first gift with a second and more appropriate one.

He held the much-discarded mirror to her face. She grimaced and started to knock it out of his feet. But wait—Who was this rosy-checked stranger grimacing back at her? She took the mirror between her trembling hands; she stared, she smiled the radiant smile of a woman whose ugliness, for the first time, has been ameliorated to mere plainness.

"Sisters," she cried. "Look at me!" The sisters looked at her and liked what they saw. One of them snatched the vial from Bin's willing legs and painted her own cheeks so generously that she resembled a Babylonian whore (much the most whorish, I am told by the Centaurs).

The vial was empty, eighteen workers remained unbeautiful. Bion pointed his feeler.

There, there, in the juniper trees, just beyond the clearing!

Work was forgotten; the workers in a body, running and skipping and flying, pursued the Telchin with raucous cries and, wonder of wonders, found him displaying not one but twenty vials of carmine, each with a mirror, as a shopkeeper displays his wares. But these wares appeared to be free.

The drones, meanwhile, had lolled on the edge of the clearing and feigned indifference to these foolish women and their ungainly pet, but now they stirred to life. They sighed and groaned to their feet; with studied indifference, they followed the tumult. Perhaps there was something for them. Sunlord paused to retrieve the original mirror and admire his reflection.

"What's going on?" The cry was shrill and not in the least melodious. Saffron had emerged from the hive. "What's happened to my workers?" She flew after them like a chicken hawk after chickens and landed among them like a particularly ravenous hawk.

Eunostos crept out of his trunk. There was no one between him and the hive.

Saffron, who had no need for carmine on her own honied skin, began to scatter the vials as if they had been clay images of forbidden gods.

"Idle adornments," she shrilled. "I turn my back and you paint yourselves like wenches. Who's going to finish the hive?"

She began to lay about her with her little fists. She kicked and cursed and stamped on vials of carmine. She bent a mirror against a trunk. Nor did she spare the drones.

"I don't expect you to work, you good-for-nothings, but you don't have to encourage the workers to your own idleness." A knee in a soft midriff. A stinging blow across a plump cheek.

But what was this? The whirlwind ceased to whirl, the dust settled. The wounded could nurse their wounds; the winded could catch their breath.

There was more than carmine and mirrors, it seemed. How had she overlooked it in her descent? A chest brimming with necklaces and armbands, rings and seal-stones! (In truth, she had not overlooked it. Bion and several friends had hastily dragged it out of the bushes while she was ranting against her workers.) Suspicious, she thrust a hand into the seeming treasure. She lifted a necklace in five tiers of jade and rose quartz and tentatively placed it around her neck. Then the innate suspicion of her race and position and her own grasping self reared its Hydra head. Something for nothing? Impossible. What did this eight-legged fellow expect from her? Wax? Honey? Perhaps herself in some barbarous interracial marriage?

Eunostos had anticipated and prepared the Telchin for just such a question. Bion pointed to her anklet, a worthless piece of tin masquerading as silver. So that was it. He had come to trade. She pretended to consider and reconsider. She feigned reluctance as she bent to unclasp it. She fondled and caressed it, presented, withdrew, and finally relinquished it in exchange for a necklace which, in the slave markets of Thebes, would have fetched a dozen stalwart Nubians or twenty nubile maidens. Then she reached into the chest and seized a tiara encrusted with amethysts and chrysolites.

Eunostos streaked for the entrance to the hive.

The roof and walls were translucent; in the filtered light of the afternoon sun, he could see his way even in rooms where there were not any candelabra to guide him. His problem was where to be guided. He did not know which passage to follow, where to twist, turn, reverse or advance. He only knew that this labyrinth was a prison as well as a home, a workshop, a place of storage, and that one of its rooms was a cell with Kora and me as its inmates. He skulked by a room where a worker was mixing pollen with honey. He ducked out of a corridor to allow two workers, a patrol, he supposed, to pass without seeing him. It was not easy to hide his six-foot bulk in so unfamiliar a place, nor to keep from scraping his horns on ceilings accommodated to the four feet of the average Thria.

Then, the scent, faint but undeniable: the loved, remembered scent of green foliage and crisp brown bark which permeates our gowns, indeed our very skins. Remember, Eunostos's mother had been a Dryad; he had loved that scent from his infancy.

He dared not call, he could only follow his nostrils, and fortunately they were keen. They began to quiver as he neared his destination. His tail lashed eagerly. He restrained a bellow. Then—his nostrils proclaimed, his heart affirmed—only a door stood between him and his beloved.

"Kora," he whispered loudly. "Zoe!"

We heard him as if he were in the room with us. "Lower your voice, Eunostos, and raise the bolt. There are no guards in here."

"There are out here!" It was not Eunostos's voice; it was the rasping buzz of a worker guard.

A struggle, a flutter, a bellow, a flurry of cries I can only call cackles. The sound of a frenziedly resistant body being dragged down corridors. It must have taken at least six of them—all the guards in the house—to overpower him.

"Zoe, Kora, they've got me! They've trussed a net!"

The acorns had renewed my strength. At Eunostos's call, I was the wolf whose cub has been caught in a hunter's net. I was the whale whose calf is threatened by sharks. I was the Mother Earth bereft of her young. I raged, I thundered, I rammed against the door with my not inconsiderable might until it creaked and threatened to yield.

"Kora, help me!" But she was already at my side and her additional strength—I would never think her frail again—snapped the bolt, which was only wood, and swung open the door. There were no guards left to stop us. We followed the sounds of the scuffle and bounded out of the house.

An alarming sight awaited us. Saffron, adorned in the many-tiered necklace, bedecked in the amethyst and chrysolite tiara, was returning to the hive, and the painted workers were fluttering dutifully but dourly after her. She saw her guards; she saw Eunostos; she did not yet see Kora and me.

"Into the pot with him!" she shouted to the guards. But he was heavy and still struggling in spite of the net; they had to heave and toil for every inch they raised him. Creature of earth, he fought to retain the earth. Their wings were shredded, their faces by his hooves.

You might not expect agility from a woman of my dimensions. You would underestimate me. After all, I have been climbing trees, with or without ladders, for three hundred and sixty years, and amplitude is not to be confused with obesity. In the twinkling of a firefly, I snatched Saffron out of the air and flung her into the vat. Before she could extricate herself, I scrambled onto the rim, seized a ladle, and swatted her on the head. Then I forced her face under the liquid.

"Let Eunostos go -or I will drown your queen," I shouted to the six guards.

The guards stared at me with disbelief. Saffron momentarily revived, sputtered to the surface, and disappeared again beneath my ladle.

They released Eunostos and let him fall the few feet they had managed to raise him from the ground. Flying in a circle around the vat, roseate still in carmine, they had ceased to look glum. They did not look fearful; in fact, they looked downright hopeful. After all, Saffron could not take away their mirrors as long as she remained in the vat.

By now Eunostos had struggled free of his net. He started to clamber up beside me. "Zoe, jump to the ground. I'll take your place."

"Get Kora to safety," I cried. "They won't hurt me while I have their queen. But I can't stay here forever."

"You won't have to," he shouted. "Moschus. Partridge. Bring on the Centaurs!"

I have never seen those horse-men, manes flying, hooves clattering in disciplined unison, gallop with more sublimity. Say what you will about their infidelities (and I am not one to say anything), they are matchless warriors. And Chiron himself had come to lead them. Chiron, the oldest Beast in the Country, five hundred years of wars and travels and wisdom and sheer, white-maned heroism. With Saffron to lead them, the workers might have attacked and resisted, flung their bamboo spears from the air or dived like eagles to claw at the Centaurs' eyes. But Saffron was still in the wax, unconscious. I ladled her out of the vat and flung her onto the ground, and the leaderless workers remained unresisting (and perhaps secretly jubilant).

I jumped to the ground and saw that Eunostos, with Kora beside him, was conferring with Chiron. They talked briefly and then Chiron advanced to address the conquered Thriae. Always forgiving when it came to women and perhaps more forgiving now that the workers had painted themselves into at least a semblance of womanhood, he announced at some length, with the stylistic flourishes and dramatic pauses characteristic of his race and suitable to his station, that neither workers nor drones would be punished, since they had only followed the orders of their queen, but that they must leave the forest by the following day.

"But your queen must remain to be tried before a court of Beasts," he concluded. "She is an evil woman who has almost caused three deaths. Moschus, bring her before me."

"Can't."

"Moschus!"

"Not unless you want her like this."

Moschus pointed; the rest of us looked. And there lay Saffron in a sheath of wax, which had hardened over her body like a shroud.

She was becomingly but unmistakably dead.

You may think me a hard, merciless woman, but she had threatened Kora and me and wanted to drown Eunostos in the vat of wax. I have never spared pity for the pitiless, especially when they die through their own misdeeds.

"I know just the place for her," I said, lifting her now somewhat weightier bulk and reentering that hateful hive.

In a deserted hive, in the hexagonal central room, there is a pedestal which is no longer without its statue. Bear Girls and young Centaurs often visit the place out of curiosity. The golden skin of Saffron shines through the wax and you might mistake her for a figure carved from amber. She is much more beautiful than in life, even with her wildly tangled hair and her staring eyes. They call her the Golden Gorgon.

When I emerged from the hive, Eunostos was pleading with Kora. He had knelt to her, all six feet of matchless Minotaur, a glory of mane and horns, of youth and might and tenderness; and she, a white lotus bending to touch his head.

"And you'll marry me then and come to live in my stump?"

"Yes, Eunostos. You saved my life."

I looked into her eyes but I did not see Eunostos. I saw her dream. I saw death.

PART TWO

AEACUS

CHAPTER VIII

EUNOSTOS's trunk resounded with preparations for the wedding. He had wanted to gather flowers and twine them above the door to his bamboo house, but no—Kora did not like them broken from their plants. The roses and columbine remained in his garden; the yellow gagea in his favorite meadow. But at least the Bears of Artemis had garlanded his windows with chains of black-eyed Susans and formed a big red heart of the berries above his door.

Eunostos himself, with help from me and the Centaurs, had prepared the feast. Tables groaned beneath baked dormice and roasted woodpeckers, honey cakes and loaves of wheaten bread sprinkled with sunflower seeds. And poor, fat Partridge had fermented a beverage of onion grass which Eunostos had accepted graciously but carefully segregated from the skins of wine and beer. The air was sweet not only with the delicacies of the table, but with fragrances from the underground workshop of the Telchins: a hint of myrrh, and intimation of sandarac, an essence of lavender, marjoram, and thyme.

Eunostos waited: it was not yet time for his friends to arrive, for friends and groom to fetch the bride from her tree, for Chiron to officiate over the ceremonies, for the wedding to be consummated in the bamboo house while we, the guests, roistered in the garden and shouted bawdy jests through the window.

Eunostos waited and, since most bridegrooms are as nervous as a Dryad at the sight of an ax, I waited with him.

"Eunostos," I said, noticing the twitch in his tail, "it's not as if you lacked experience. A Bee queen and all those Dryads—you haven't a thing to fear."

"But Kora is so—ethereal," he said.

I was getting a little tired of Kora's ethereality. "Treat her like any other woman. It's just what she needs."

"Eunostos, Zoe, did you hear the news?" It was Partridge,

puffing more than usual.

"How do we know if we've heard it unless you tell us?"

"A Man, a Cretan. Right here in the country. Wandered in between the cliffs. Wounded, too!"

"He's broken the covenant," I said. "Chiron will be furious."

"He's probably in a daze," Eunostos said, doubtless remembering his own recent wounds. "Zoe, will you stay here to greet my guests? I'm going to help him."

"On your wedding day?"

"What if you hadn't helped me when the Panisci beat me up?"

"Oh, very well," I grumbled. I am not as heartless as I sound. I remembered Kora's dream.

*   *   *   *

Aeacus, brother of Minos, king of Crete, sighed in the palace courtyard and dipped his hand in a pool of silver fish. Palm trees leaned above him, drooping their fronds like great green birds with many wings. Saffron crocuses rippled a golden fleece. Egyptians live in the past: they look at the Pyramids and yearn for departed majesties. Achaeans live in the future: they look at their bronze-heeled chariots and yearn for tomorrow's battle. But Cretans live in the moment, poised like a blue lotus on the stilled waters of time, perfectly content, untroubled by memory or anticipation; a joyous people. And Aeacus till now had been the happiest as well as the handsomest of princes, with all the prerogatives and none of the burdens of royalty.

But Aeacus sighed, and a lady of the court, Metope, looked at him in astonishment. She was abloom in a flaring skirt and brandished her bare breasts like melons ripe to be plucked.

"Aeacus," she said. "Tonight the ladies of the court will dance the Dance of the Cranes beside the River Kairatos. And afterwards they will choose their lovers from the men who have come to watch them. Do you want to come?"

"No."

"No!" she repeated, incredulous. "You no longer find me pleasurable?"

"At the moment nothing pleases me."

"Cruel Aeacus! You speak like a Hittite instead of a Cretan. Have I developed a wrinkle since I last looked in my mirror?"

He peered into her face and detected a faint little network of lines beneath her eyes. But this time he remembered to speak like a Cretan instead of a Hittite.

"No, dear Metope, there are no new wrinkles. Nor old ones. The fault lies with me, not you. Your face is as smooth and pink as the inside of a conch shell, and much more soft. Lately I've been—somewhere else."

"Where, Aeacus? Where would you rather be than Knossos? Thebes, Memphis, Babylon...?"

"I don't know."

"Come to the dance then. It will bring you back to us. It will make you laugh again."

"Very well, I will come."

He was not affronted by her invitation. In Knossos, the women were as bold and amorous as the men. Besides, he had already lain with her in a meadow of asphodels and on a stone couch mountained with pillows and called her, in flattering light and under the influence of wine, a mortal incarnation of the Great Mother.

He shook himself free of his sighs and laughed. "Yes, I will come.

She looked at him with a frank, level gaze of a race whose women hold equal footing with men. "Laughter becomes you. It shows your teeth, which are white like the shells on the beach. You make me think of abundance, of pomegranates in a luxuriant field. We're small, we Cretans. Yet there's still a richness about you. It's more than your bronze chest and roseate cheeks. More than your lyre-sweet laughter. More than your supple hands, so full of gifts for the children of the court. You yourself are a gift, the rarest of all. Did you know that you are loved above your brother?"

"That is very wrong," he said. "My brother is king." He felt the affront to his brother's dignity. Still, he had to admit that it was good to be loved. He, who loved purple of murex, blue-gray of dolphin, laughter of harvesters returning from the barley field. He who was only angry at ugliness or when the Achaeans raided the Cretan coast. Yes, he loved to be loved. He basked in love like a cat in a palace lightwell.

"Your brother is king, but there is something almost Egyptian about him. He thinks too much."

"And I?"

"You feel. That is what it means to be Cretan."

He lifted one of the curls from her forehead and kissed her lightly on her white skin, which curls and cosmetics and parasols protected from the hot Cretan sun.

"I will watch the Dance of the Cranes," he said, and he followed her with his eyes as she moved, prettily but absurdly like a great crimson flower, through a doorway flanked by stone bulls and into the palace. Then he forgot her.

He sighed and fled from the court, down gypsum stairs, across a second courtyard paved with cobblestones and worn by dancing feet, along the triumphal approach to the palace, and between trellises of grapes and on…and yet on… Behind him, the track of a goat through silver-leafed olive trees. He could not have told where he ran or why, till he stood in a tamarisk grove and leaned on a tree to stifle a sob—and to listen.

The tree was speaking to him. It was not that she spoke in words, she spoke to his heart. She welcomed him. But then, it was widely known that the Mother loved trees and bushes and flowers as animals and endowed the lowliest plant with indwelling spirit, perhaps invisible, perhaps as tangible as Metope in her poppy-shaped skirt. Aeacus knew, of course, about those very tangible spirits known as Dryads, but he also knew that they dwelt in the Country of the Beasts, and no Cretan invaded those forbidden fastnesses of Minotaurs and Centaurs and other horrendous beings sometimes spied by those who ventured to the edge of the forest (for that is the view which the Cretans hold of us).

Dryads lived in oak trees. And yet this tamarisk tree made a strange whispering, like a tongue guessed at but not quite understood, like a soft-voiced maiden from the Misty Isles, whispering at her loom; and somehow he felt companioned by her.

"Tree," he whispered. "Have you something to say to me?"

The tree did not answer him, but he saw in the eyes of his mind an image of other trees, in other places, immemorial cedars on the slopes of great limestone mountains, fir trees, prickly but not wounding, and one tall oak which spread its limbs like enfolding wings.

"My brother." It was Minos himself, the king. "I saw you start from the palace like a wounded gazelle and followed you here." The king was a man of thirty with a youthful, unlined face but hair as white as the snow atop Mt. Ida; diminutive like all of his race but august from his plumed headdress to his feet shod in high boots of Egyptian antelope leather. Born as blithe as his people, he had tried to retain their lightness and their laughter. But even the king of a happy people has cares. He was ready to wrestle the bull or go to the theater where maidens danced with a python in their arms, but he must also wrestle at times with the problems of ruling a populous empire whose ships sailed as far as the Misty Isles to bring back tin and dye.

"What troubles my little brother?" he repeated, with the tenderness of an older brother who would always see the younger as little, though they were identical in height. There was also perplexity in his voice and a gentle reproach. "You come to the grove—alone. You speak to the trees, when you might better speak to your brother and king. Is it for love you pine? Never before has a maiden disdained the handsomest of men."

"No, my brother. It is none of these things."

"What then?"

What then? It was a question without an answer. "I don't know," he said sadly. "I felt a kind of want."

"For every want there is an answer. The thirsty man drinks wine from the nearest cellar. The hungry man eats lobster from the Great Green Sea. The lovelorn man makes love to a woman old in experience but young in beauty."

Aeacus forced a smile. "How could I thirst or hunger or yearn after love in many-pleasured Crete? I'm acting like a foolish schoolboy who has broken his tablets and forgotten his lessons. If I could only understand…"

The king appeared to muse. "Not so foolish, perhaps. Our ancestors were a restless people before they settled in Crete. Perhaps one is speaking through you. And I have the answer. Last night an Achaean warship raided the coast. Three farmhouses were burned. Our patrol craft rammed and sank her, but there's still a raiding party afoot. They've gone inland. There's no end to the mischief they can do."

"I'll go after them. I'll pick some men from the palace guard and—"

"Only if you so will it. There is no need for a prince to endanger himself in pursuit of pirates unless he chooses. I have already chosen a party, and the head of the palace guard can lead them."

"I will lead them."

The king smiled. Through the intertwined limbs of the feathery tamarisk trees, a sunbeam smote his hair and kindled its white to silver. He was crowned more truly than with his royal headdress. "Very well, you shall lead them. Your skill with the bulls is legend. Your dagger flashes like a dragonfly. But take care. Remember that Cretan agility and daggers are more than a match for Achaean brawn and swords—but only if you take care. You must leave your sighs in the palace, or an ill-smelling braggart will put a sword through your heart before you remember to draw your dagger."

"I've been poor company of late, haven't I, my brother?"

"It is true that a sad Cretan is no asset to a happy court. If you stay in your present mind, you'll have the ladies in tears, and their cheeks will be streaked with kohl. Go to the hills and find your lost laughter."

The brothers embraced each other with more than ritual formality. Aeacus loved Minos above all other men. To other races, he knew—the solemn Egyptians, the vainglorious Babylonians—the Cretans seemed light and fickle, incapable of deep, enduring love, because their funerals resembled festivals and they rarely shed tears. To a Cretan, however, death was not oblivion but another country, where all that one loved, all those one loved, were restored and immortalized beneath the radiant smiles of the Great Mother and her Griffin Judge. Yes, the Cretans could love, and if they fell into love as easily as a child falls into a sand pit and climbed out with neither bruises nor scratches, it was not from fickleness, Aeacus would have argued, but abundance of affection. Aeacus himself loved thirty friends, uncountable women and even more children, his brother, himself, and most of all, the someone or something he had not yet found.

The chase led inland, upward, away from the salt-sweet wind of the sea and toward the mountains which ridged the island like an exposed backbone. Burning farmhouses…slaughtered sheep…a rooster crowing incessantly from the top of an olive tree… Thus the marauders had branded the earth in passing. Such raids were becoming more frequent now that the Cretan ships had so many colonies to visit, so little time to guard their own coastline with its innumerable indentations, its coves and projections and rocky headlands, its perfection of concealment.

But the Achaeans were still regarded as a minor annoyance, the price of empire. If anyone anticipated a wholesale invasion by those blond, awkward, sword-wielding barbarians, he kept such foolish anticipations from the king. A minor annoyance except, Aeacus mused, to the fishermen or the country folk who lost their houses and often their lives and had not the consolation of a fixed, firm faith, but only a body of shapeless superstitions in which the Underworld loomed as a dark and sinister habitat of monsters and monstrous torments.

It was not often that Aeacus thought of fishermen and farmers. They existed; they provided the court with fish, meat, vegetables, fruit, olive oil, and wool; they performed the function designated for them in the scheme of the Great Mother. Did they love? Did they sorrow? He felt a twinge of guilt that he so rarely thought of them, then the guilt of feeling guilty when he was the king's beloved brother embarked upon a gallant adventure, and then the happy abandonment of a race not given to introspection.

A small child came running to them across a field. Behind him, smoke billowed from a wattle hut, hens collided with pigs and sought refuge in a torn vineyard. The child, a lean little boy of perhaps five, was weeping with uncontrollable tears. Aeacus lifted him in his arms and felt the beating heart and waited patiently till the boy could speak.

"Mama and papa..."

"Dead, my child?"

"Yes."

"Don't cry, don't cry." Strange, the sight of tears. No one cried in the court. Or at least they hid their tears. "My men will give them a proper burial. They'll be waiting for you in the Underworld. The Griffin Judge will appraise them kindly and watch over them and keep them safe."

"Will he?" The child looked up at him with astonishment. He was ugly, almost monkeylike in his small brown leanness.

In the court of Knossos, such ugliness might have repelled him. Not now. Not here. "I thought it was only the great lords like you he watched over."

"It's everyone." He spoke with assurance, but until that moment had never considered if peasants, like kings and courtiers, went to the Underworld. Was there room for them? Did they continue to serve their earthly masters?

"And one of my men will stay with you till we come back, and then we will find a home for you closer to a town, where you will be safe."

The child clung to him with the tenacity of the animal he resembled. Aeacus had to disengage his fingers, gently but firmly, and hand him to one of his men. He would have liked to stay in the ruined house, bury the parents with the proper services (wherever their ghosts might roam), feed the child, and tell him stories of friendly dolphins and dog-headed fish. When I return to the court, he told himself, I will wed and have a child. Many children. Perhaps it was for them I have sighed, for my unborn children. The tree had whispered of—something.

*   *   *   *

An hour's march from where he had left the boy, in the midst of a rocky, pitted meadow, he met the Achaeans. The pits disgorged warriors, the rocks came to life, and the little Cretans found themselves beleaguered before they could draw their daggers.

Draw them they did at last, and then it was an equal fight. Like blue monkeys beset by dogs, they fought the big-bodied, blond intruders, nimbly sidestepping their sword thrusts, thrusting with their own daggers, until a single Achaean limped from the field, and Aeacus stood alone among his fallen men, too tired to give chase, scarcely strong enough to support his own weight, wounded—if not to death—at least to a dazed benumbment.

He looked at his slain friends in the midst of the field and looked around him dazedly and saw that he was not far from two great cliffs with a forest narrowed between them like a wedge. He caught the healing fragrance of bark and oak leaves and heard the faint rustling of water. Perhaps he could find a stream and bathe his wounds and return to bury his friends. Could he walk so far?

Dimly he recognized the forest. The Country of the Beasts, where no Cretan ventured, half from fear and half from remembering a covenant made before the beginning of recorded time, before there had been any scribes to scratch history on clay tablets, that this one forest belonged inviolably and eternally to the Beasts.

Still, the trees whispered to him: cone-shaped cypresses, smoothed and sculptured as if by the nimble fingers of the Great Mother, and tumultuous oaks whose branches seemed little jungles. "You may break the covenant," they seemed to say. "Enter our deepest shadows and learn our mysteries and yes, our terrors, but even terror can be beautiful."

The sun gaped like a wound; the limbs were succoring hands which comforted and promised to heal even while they threatened to hold.

He stumbled into the forest.

He lay on the ground, eyes closed, poised between sleep and waking. He heard the rustle of bushes. Painfully he opened his eyes and saw a young boy, no, a young bull. No, a brawny bullboy with silken red hair punctuated by horns. He tried to raise his hand. The boy stepped back from him with evident alarm.

"I can't get up," Aeacus said. He lay in his own blood and wondered with more curiosity than fear if he were going to die. The boy circled him, approached, confirmed his helplessness, and spoke in a deep but musical Cretan.

"Shall I help you up?"

Aeacus deliberated. "I don't know. I might start to bleed again. Perhaps you could first bind my wounds."

"Let *me* bind your wounds."

She had come so quietly that Aeacus and evidently the Minotaur boy (for that seemed to be his race) had not even heard her approach. She had come through the trees, or out of a tree, it was hard to say. She was taller than Cretan ladies and she wore, in place of their bell-shaped skirts and open bodices, a loose flowing gown the color of leaves and a necklace of orange berries. Her hair was green like her gown, swept above her head in a knot, and held by a silver pin in the shape of a grasshopper. Her ears, thus revealed, were delicately pointed. The boy looked at her with surprise and doubt.

"We can take him to my house," he said.

"Mine is closer, Eunostos. But first I must clean his wounds." She knelt beside him and touched damp moss to a cut on his shoulder. The relief was immediate, but whether from the moss or the administering hand, he could not be sure.

"And what shall *I* do?" asked the Minotaur boy, seemingly aggrieved at being replaced as the rescuer of this wounded stranger. Aeacus liked him.

"After he has rested," she said, "you shall help me carry him to my house. We shall make a litter from sticks and vines and carry him as hunters carry a stag, though much more gently, of course."

"What is your name?" Aeacus asked.

"I am Kora, the Dryad."

"And where is your house?"

"In a tree. Where else?" she laughed.

Aeacus closed his eyes, assured of his rescue and unashamed of his helplessness, since there is nothing more welcome to helpful people than those who need to be helped. It was not long until the girl and the Minotaur boy had fashioned the litter and his body swayed to their gliding steps as they carried him into the forest, into the Country of the Beasts.

In spite of his wounds, he did not sigh.

CHAPTER IX

IN EUNOSTOS's absence, I greeted his guests and tried to put them at ease. Here was Partridge, heading at once for the skin of fermented onion juice and avoiding the other guests with the zeal of one whose conversation was limited to "huh" and "can't" and "don't know." Here was Bion, hovering at the door as though he were not sure of his right to mingle with the higher orders of Beast; after all, there were those who considered him a mere domestic. I took him at once to the largest table and soon he was clutching a loaf of wheaten bread between his forelegs and happily bobbing his head. And Moschus—surely I would have trouble with Moschus, who always arrived drunk and began his amorous advances with his salutations. Tonight he was drunker than usual and accompanied by an uninvited guest, no friend of Eunostos, a frowsy young Dryad of about fifty.

"There are more birds on the limb than one," he smirked to me, proceeded to fling a large beerskin over his shoulder, and retired with his friend to the garden.

"Yes, cuckoos," I called after him.

There were Centaur boys who clamored to see Eunostos's workshop, though they could not climb his ladder and had to content themselves with peering into the shadows at the work-bench, the tools, a chair without legs, the embryo of a table. There were Bears of Artemis who had to be coaxed out of corners with compliments on how artistically they had strung the black-eyed Susans, and—But why bore you with a list of the guests? Eunostos had innumerable friends; he had only excluded Panisci (except for Partridge) and Thriae.

But all the time I was worrying about Eunostos and waiting for him to return, and feeling that the Cretan could not have chosen a worse day in the year to invade the forest, even if he was wounded, and Chiron ought to exile him as soon as he had recovered his strength.

Just about dusk, Eunostos walked in the door as if he had forgotten it was his own wedding day, looking puzzled, troubled, and solitary.

But of course everyone hailed him as the happy bridegroom and in the next breath wanted to know about the Cretan. Some had glimpsed him but no one had dared to speak to him. Being a Man, he was presumed to be dangerous.

"Weren't you scared, Eunostos?"

"Is it true he doesn't have horns or hooves or fur or *anything?*"

"Did he soft-talk you and then try to slip a knife between your ribs?"

"He was badly hurt," said Eunostos. "Kora took him to her house to nurse his wounds." The guests remained quiet, waiting for details; waiting in vain.

"But the wedding," I cried at last. "It's time for us to go and summon the bride from her tree!"

"She said we were to go on with the feasting without her. Pretend it was a festival to the Great Mother or something. The wedding will have to wait a day or two. Otherwise, the Cretan may die."

There was a babble of voices. No bride? No wedding? Kora nursing a *Man?*

"Shut up and don't spoil the party," Moschus whinnied from the garden. "When Kora's ready, we'll have another feast at my house." (Moschus had never been known to give—or miss—a feast.)

At the first chance, I led Eunostos into the flower garden (Moschus and his friend were sprawled among the vegetables). He had a curious look about him. An old look in young eyes.

"What is he like, this Cretan?"

"A little fellow, but manly. There were wounds all over him but he never complained once. I liked him."

"What did he *look* like, Eunostos?"

"Like a prince, I'd say. His loincloth was purple, with a silver clasp on the belt. And his face—it was somehow royal."

"Eunostos, see to your guests, will you? I've drunk enough and talked enough for a year. My ankles are killing me." I left him standing with his hand on Bion's head.

But I did not return to my tree, I went to Kora's tree. Myrrha was downstairs fondling the bridal robe, bright as a field of goldenrod, in which she had married her Centaur and which she had taken out of a cedar chest and freshened with myrrh for Kora. She started talking at once.

"I told the girl to go ahead and get married. That I would look after the young Man. But now, you would think she's the only Dryad in the Country who knows how to treat a wound. And she even sent me down here! Said he needed to sleep and mustn't be disturbed by female chatter. That from my own daughter."

"Well, he's going to hear a little female chatter now," I said, charging up the stairs in spite of Myrrha's protest.

He was lying on Kora's couch, faintly smiling, eyes closed; sleeping comfortably but needing his sleep, from the look of his wounds. Still, they were obviously not going to kill him, and Myrrha, for all of her frivolity, knew the right remedies and could have been left to nurse him even at the price of missing her daughter's wedding.

Kora was sitting on the floor beside the couch. She had not begun to dress for the wedding; she was wearing a simple brown tunic, caught at the waist with a sash of grapevine, and her hair for once needed a comb. She saw me and put a finger to her lips. I seized her hand and pulled her after me into the little hall at the head of the stairs. A single window, hardly large enough for a woodpecker to confuse with his nest, admitted a slender beam of moonlight.

"I'm not going to wake your precious friend," I said, "but I am going to give you a piece of my mind. Such a thing to tell your groom! To have the wedding feast without you! If you don't trust your mother to look after this interloper, what about me? I was mixing potions and simples long before you were born, and I have a lighter touch than you might suppose from the size of my hands. You can still join Eunostos and have the wedding."

"No." That was all. Silent Kora.

"No what? I think you had better qualify that answer."

"I found him, Zoe. I brought him home. He's my responsibility."

"I thought we were talking about Eunostos. As for your Cretan, nonsense. Partridge found him first anyway. Does that make him Partridge's responsibility? He's lucky to find anyone to look after him since he broke the covenant."

"But I called him here."

I felt as if the fire in my brazier had died on a bleak winter night. "You mean—"

"In one of the dreams I told you about, there was a young Cretan. I tried to call out to him. I didn't think he heard. But he did. And came. And when he lay wounded in the forest, *he* called to me."

"Did he say that?"

"He doesn't need to say it."

I seized her shoulders and shook her as if she were a naughty child who had robbed a swallow's nest. "You'd better think what you're going to tell Eunostos."

*   *   *   *

Chiron had come and, finding no bride to marry, returned to his compound with injured dignity. The Bears of Artemis had long since retired to their hollow logs and bed. Moschus, his new conquest caught in a tangle of arms and legs which might charitably be called an embrace, was snoring among the vegetables. Partridge, rotund with onion juice, drowsed under one of the tables. Bion was gathering fallen scraps to hoard in his workshop.

Eunostos scratched Bion's head. "You'll look after things while I go to see Kora, won't you, old friend?" He was taking her a basket of grapes.

Bion's look was questioning: shall I come too and carry the basket?

"No, I'd better go alone. Too many of us might disturb the Cretan." He looked behind him at the fallen garlands, the swaying lanterns which lit only sleep, the revelers who had reveled without a bride. I won't come back until I come with Kora, he thought.

It was early morning when he arrived at Kora's tree. Myrrha, who had just entertained and dismissed a Centaur on his way home from the feast, met him with a sleepy greeting.

"Kora sat up all night with the Cretan. She's still awake and you can go right up to her room."

He found that she had propped Aeacus's head on a cushion and was feeding him a warm posset of fennel leaves steeped in sparrow broth. She and Aeacus turned to Eunostos when he entered the room. Aeacus smiled. There was a gash in his left leg which Kora had dressed with moss, and several scars on his chest, and one above his right eye. He must have been in pain but you would not have known from his smile.

"It's the Minotaur boy," he cried. "I've wanted to thank you but I've been asleep." He started to rise from the couch, but Kora pushed him back against the cushion.

"I brought you some grapes," said Eunostos to Kora, then to her guest. "For you too, sir."

She stood above the couch like a warm green flame; her cheeks were flushed and her hair, usually swept above her head, tumbled over her shoulders in a sweet abandonment. Strangely, she was crying. No sobs shook her body, but tears streamed down her cheeks. She was radiance troubled with shadows.

She may be crying for the Cretan, Eunostos told himself, and looked at Aeacus to see if his condition had worsened since they had found him in the forest. But he looked much better than he had the previous day; he was clearly improving, in spite of his multiple wounds, and enjoying good spirits, except that he too saw Kora's tears and his smile became astonishment and then dismay. He caught and pressed her hand and she gripped his fingers with a frantic yearning. And then Eunostos knew that she was not crying for Aeacus but for him, because she had found her dream.

He dropped the basket of grapes and stumbled down the stairs.

"Eunostos," Myrrha greeted him as he flung aside the curtain in the door. "You hardly spoke on your way up. Isn't he 'a handsome young man? Eunostos—"

*   *   *   *

When I left Kora's tree, I did not return to Eunostos's wedding party. How could I tell the groom that his bride had forsaken him for a Man? Kora must tell him; Kora must make her peace with him. I returned to my tree and tried to sleep. I alternated between tossing on my couch and walking to a window to look at the moondusted oak trees, Kora's faintly visible at some distance, and the field of flowers where Eunostos had written his poems and dreamed of a Dryad to love him.

Then, the sun was a faint presentiment behind the trees, and a creeping of yellow back into the flowers, and belated sleep for me.

Someone touched my shoulder. "Zoe."

"Go away. I just got to sleep."

"Zoe, please!"

"Eunostos!"

He fell to his knees and buried his head in my bosom. I ran my hand through his mane. "You've come from Kora."

"Yes."

"And she told you."

"What am I to do, Aunt Zoe?"

"Wait, my dear." I had no wisdom for him; only platitudes; only a tenderness which welled into my heart like hot water into a Cretan bath, wounding even while it warmed.

"For what?"

"Another Kora. A worthier Kora."

"I'm never going to love again."

"Everyone does. If they let themselves."

"You do, Aunt Zoe, but you're different from me. You can fall out of love."

"I don't fall out of love, I just add one love onto another and keep them all, and so will you."

"No," he said. "There's only Kora."

How could I tell him that what he felt for her was as sharply hurtful as the thrust of a Thriae spear but not beyond healing? The Kora he loved lived only in his poems; it was his misfortune that he expected her soul to equal her beauty. Her soul was not unbeautiful, but being young had not had time to match her face.

"We'll see, my dear. Meanwhile, do you want to stay with your Aunt Zoe awhile? You don't have to go back to that lonely house yet. Bion and I will clean it for you and have it waiting."

"I'd better go back. It's all I've got."

"Perhaps," I said, "you have more than you think," but he had already left the room, and I heard my ladder sagging under his weight, and the thump of his hooves on the ground, and the slow, sad steps toward his house.

No one has ever seen me cry. I choose my times.

Three days had passed. Eunostos sat at his workbench with a saw in his hand. But the saw was idle, the hand did not move, and the chair which he had begun before the proposed wedding remained a mere beginning. Bion prodded him with a feeler. It was Partridge who had brought him material for the chair as a wedding gift: tanned oxhide to be stretched across a framework of willow rods. It was Bion who had brought him the tools. Partridge had gone in search of his dinner, since Eunostos would not allow him to graze in his garden, but Bion had remained to keep him company. Eunostos stroked his head and never noticed that his friend was too miserable to wave his antennae.

*   *   *   *

Someone called his name. Someone was wandering in his garden and looking for him, but did not seem to know the location of the workshop, whose entrance was hidden by a blackberry thicket to discourage Panisci or Thriae. He had better confront his visitor before his roses were trampled.

He climbed the earthen staircase and stepped into the sunshine. It was so bright, after the pale lanterns of his workshop, that he blinked, and only then did he recognize the visitor.

Aeacus.

"I thought you were wounded," he growled.

"I was—I still am. This is my first day out of the tree. I wanted to talk to you."

At the sight of his limp, Eunostos stifled an urge to butt him. He did not want to talk to Aeacus. He did not want to look at his kindly smile, at the kind violet eyes. He wished that Aeacus had looked smug and condescending, or arrogant and boastful, and then he might have butted him in spite of the limp.

But Aeacus breathed heavily and leaned his weight on a trellis where wild roses were twining tentative feelers.

"You're about to knock down my trellis. Kora wouldn't like that. She says roses have souls."

"Forgive me. Kora should know." His pain was evident when he tried to stand without support. The wound in his leg had hardly begun to heal.

Eunostos pointed toward his house. "There are chairs inside."

"It looks like a crown of bamboo. Light and airy and graceful. Did you build it yourself?"

"Yes, but the Centaurs brought me the bamboo."

They sat facing each other, silent, and Aeacus lost his smile. He looked sad and perplexed, though his bronzed little body glittered in his murex-purple loincloth, with its silver clasp in the shape of a halcyon bird.

At first they carefully avoided a direct discussion of Kora.

"Chiron is going to let me stay in the forest," Aeacus said. "I've broken the covenant but only by accident. However, if I stay, it must be for good. I can't go back to Knossos and expect to return here. People might want to follow me, and where would the covenant be?"

"And you've accepted his conditions?"

"Yes." The answer was strangely subdued. He paused. "Till you came with the grapes," he said, staring at the fountain as it cascaded above the seashell castle, "I didn't know that Kora had promised to marry you. I thought you were just her friend. Like a younger brother. I wanted you to be my friend too. Since I woke up in the forest and you were there to help me—well, I've *liked* you."

"I don't believe you."

"Why else would I come here now?"

"I believe you then, but I still don't like you."

"Of course you don't. But I hope you will in time. When you understand."

Why did older people—Men as well as Beasts, it seemed, even dear Zoe—always talk about understanding as if it came with years? He understood well enough at fifteen; he was rough and graceless and Kora had preferred a prince from a glamorous city. He understood but he still hurt.

Helplessly he pointed to the house and the garden. "I made it for her. The house is bamboo, but it's right in the middle of a hollow oak trunk so she could have left her tree and lived here with me. Dryads can change oaks, you know. Now there's nobody to share it with."

But Bion was standing in the door and Eunostos saw that the Telchin had heard him and his feelers had wilted with disappointment.

"I didn't mean you," Eunostos cried, jumping to his hooves and leading Bion into the room. "But you have your own workshop and relatives. I meant somebody to stay with me all the time."

"I think you have a lot of friends," said Aeacus. "Zoe says you're the nicest Beast in the country and I had better consider myself lucky if you'll even speak to me. I think you can have as much company as you want." He held out a coaxing hand to Bion, but the Telchin scuttled away from his touch and retreated into the garden.

"Not Kora."

"Kora too. She does love you, Eunostos, but not in the way you want. She can't help herself. I couldn't help coming to her, and I can't help staying now that I know she wants me."

"You've fallen in love with her in just three days? I've known her all my life."

"I've always been in love with her. At least, with someone like her I was waiting to meet. The Great Mother arranges these things, and all we mortals can do is accept gracefully if we lose, and graciously if we gain."

"I'm not very graceful. My hooves are clumsy and I would trip on my own tail if it reached to the ground."

"Kora says she loves you better than anyone in the whole forest next to me. She says you saved her life and wrote poems to her and made her feel that her beauty was something precious, and not a worthless, empty shell. I wish—I wish—"

Eunostos had not expected to see an eloquent Cretan groping for words. He wanted to hate or at least dislike this Man who had stolen his bride, but he could not stay angry except with a wicked and heartless person like Saffron. It would seem that Aeacus had not intended to wrong him and that he was truly ashamed. Otherwise, why had he left his couch before he was well and walked through the forest to bring his apologies?

"Well," said Aeacus, straining to his feet. "I must let you get back to your shop. But I warn you, I'm coming again soon, and going to keep on coming until you become my friend!"

He swayed and started to fall. Eunostos caught him and settled him into the chair.

"Now stay there," he ordered as gruffly as he could. "I'm going to get you some catnip tea. Zoe says it will cure anything."

In the next room, he kindled the coals on the hearth and sprinkled some dried leaves in a pan of water. "Damn," he muttered. "Great-Mother-damn." Here he was taking care of the last person in the world he wanted as a friend, and it was quite impossible to dislike anyone in your care.

When the tea had come to a boil, he poured it into a large clay cup like a turtle shell, sweetened it with honey, tasted it to make sure that it was not too hot, and carried it to Aeacus, who had to hold the cup in both of his hands, they were trembling so much. He seemed to be having a chill.

"You'll have to spend the night," said Eunostos decisively. "I'll leave Bion to look after you, and I'll go and tell Kora where you are. If you want anything, just ask Bion. But speak slowly and use simple words, and make sure that you have his attention."

"I have a feeling he doesn't like me," said Aeacus with a certain apprehension.

"That's on my account," said Eunostos. "Telchins are very loyal friends to the higher races of Beast. It's only each other they eat."

"But I'm not a Beast at all, much less higher!"

"No, but you're close enough. He likes more sinewy meat. Besides, I've left him some hazelnuts in the workshop. Now we've got to get you into the next room and onto the couch."

It was surprising how easy it was to lift a grown Man, if the

Man was a Cretan and the lifter was a Minotaur. When Aeacus, cup still clutched between his hands, lay on the couch, Eunostos propped his head on a pillow so that he could finish drinking and threw a coverlet over him. He remembered how his mother had looked after him when he had caught hoof and mouth disease from the Centaur colts.

"Is there anything I can get you before I go? Something to eat? A scroll to read? I have *Hoofbeats in Babylon, The Indiscretions of a Dryad, Centaur Songs*—"

"Anything you've written?"

"I'm not collected yet. I was planning a little scroll of poems for Kora, but they're still on palm leaves."

"Not a thing then. I'll just lie here and enjoy your house. Did you call this drink tea? We don't have it in Knossos. Beer and wine, but not tea."

"The Centaurs learned how to make it from the Yellow Men."

"It's very good. I feel better already."

"I had better go now."

"I saw the turtle in your fountain. I had a turtle till I was fifteen. He lived in a pool with silver fish."

"What happened to him?"

"He crawled away. An earthquake had made a small fissure in the wall of the courtyard. I never filled it in, hoping he would crawl back. But he didn't."

"Well, I expect he knew where he was going."

"The adjacent courtyard opened onto the street. I always hoped he was rescued by a child. Wagons aren't allowed in Knossos, so he couldn't have been run over."

"You must have missed him a great deal."

"I did. Eunostos?"

"Yes?"

Aeacus held out his hand in the universal gesture of good fellowship.

"Damn," muttered Eunostos, but he took the hand, which

was cold, shaking, and very tenacious. Reluctantly he returned the pressure. The worst had happened. He had become friends with the Man who had taken his bride. I'll end up giving them my turtle for a wedding present, he thought.

CHAPTER X

WHEN I HEARD that Eunostos and Aeacus had become friends, I thought: Well, good for Eunostos. Now he can be reconciled with Kora too and be at peace with himself. Now he can see her without illusions and love her as she really is, with her mortal limitations. For if a person rejects us and we never see him again, we suppose him larger than life, we find the fault in ourselves, and we always think: "If only I had been worthier…" But the married Kora, engaged in her daily domesticities, was a beautiful, kindhearted, but unremarkable young Dryad of flesh and green blood.

Much to his credit, Eunostos did not act like a young calf mooning over his lost love. He was nearly sixteen now; he was definitely a bull and he acted with commendable maturity. Never a worshipful look, never a whispered compliment, but always the open, bluff affection of the brother Kora seemed to want.

Kora reciprocated with a quiet gratitude. She had won a brother as well as a husband. Accompanied by Aeacus, she visited Eunostos's house and showed him how to deepen the color of his roses or train them to climb his trellis. She brought him roasted acorns and tidied his workshop and wove him a loincloth like the one Aeacus had worn when he came to the forest, green instead of purple, but just as princely, with a belt and a silver clasp in the shape of a turtle.

At that time, Aeacus never showed the least jealousy. Perhaps, knowing himself adored by Kora, he felt no need to be jealous. Besides, he liked Eunostos. It was soon a familiar sight to see the two of them exploring the forest, with Eunostos acting as guide and pointing out landmarks. Here was the hive of the Bee Queen Amber ("Watch out for her. They say she's meaner than Saffron, the one who kidnapped Kora"). Here were the log lairs of the Bear Girls—you could tell by the briar patch which they had trained to circle them like a wall and keep out predatory bears.

They hunted together too with bow and arrow or blowgun—woodpeckers, sparrows, and rabbits for the table—but Eunostos explained that they must never kill the larger animals like deer and bears.

"They're too much like us," he said. "We only kill the small ones because we have to eat. Or wolves, because they like to eat us."

Aeacus in turn taught Eunostos the uses of a dagger: how to dart and duck and thrust, how to wound, and, if necessary, to kill.

"You can even take on a man with a sword and twice your size. Small as I am, if I were to use a sword against an Achaean, I would stand as much chance as a sparrow against a hawk. The sword would weigh me down and he would slice off my head with his first good blow. But with a dagger, I'm more than a match for him. When he swings, I'm already somewhere else, usually stabbing him between the ribs."

Eunostos was too courteous to explain that he was not likely to meet anyone twice his size, that he preferred a sword to a dagger, and that what he would really like was a double-edged battle ax, which his ancestors had used against the Centaurs before the two races became friends.

Lithe-limbed little Cretan and robust, red-maned Minotaur: unlikely friends in a friendly forest.

Needless to say, Eunostos did not neglect his other friends in favor of Aeacus. He called almost daily at my tree.

"Have you gotten over her?" I asked him one day. We were on our way to Centaur Town, I to visit with Moschus (yes, we were keeping company again), he to trade a small wooden chest he had made for seeds and farm implements, since he was enlarging his garden.

He thought before he answered. "No, I just love her differently."

"What is she like to you now, Eunostos?"

"Like a hand loom. She's part of her house, part of her tree, quiet but industrious."

"No longer mysterious? No longer a goddess?"

"Not any more. But I don't mind. Now I don't have to be shy with her."

"And Aeacus. How does he see her?"

"I expect he still sees her as a goddess. You see, she's so quiet with him that he can think her into anything he likes." He might have been talking about himself before he lost Kora.

"And he's still a god to her?"

"Oh, yes."

"And to you?"

"A good friend. I like to go hunting with him. He only kills when he needs something to eat, and then nothing big like a deer or a bear. And he tells me about the palace at Knossos, and his brother, the king, who sits on a throne flanked by two stone griffins."

"Eunostos, today you sound as old and wise as Chiron. No more poems. No more reposing among the flowers." But I suspected and hoped that the old Eunostos, the young Eunostos, still lingered beneath his new serious mien.

"I had to grow up fast," he admitted.

"But not too fast to have a little fun, I hope. You have a long time in which to be old. I'll bet you haven't been wenching since—"

"Not since I fell in love with Kora," he admitted. "But don't worry. I haven't forgotten how. It's like learning to count on an abacus. You never forget."

He held out his hand and a butterfly, the large yellow kind with black markings on his wings, settled as if he had found a flower.

"Here," he said. "Here's a sunbeam for you. But don't brush the dust off his wings." He gave a tilt with his hand and the butterfly flew to me.

"You ought to save him for Kora."

His green eyes grew wide with mischief. "She doesn't need a thing."

"No?"

"She's going to have a baby!"

"A baby? But Eunostos, how wonderful!" Kora had already told me, but I let Eunostos think that he was breaking the news.

"I wasn't supposed to tell. It sort of slipped out."

"I'm glad it did. You know, I've had a bit of practice at midwifery. I delivered several of my own children without any help from anyone. I wouldn't trust Myrrha, bless her heart, to deliver a blue monkey. She would talk it back into its mother's womb. Is Aeacus pleased?"

Eunostos looked puzzled. "I really don't know. He loves children, but he hasn't had much to say about this one. In fact he's taken to going off in the forest by himself. I saw him one day at the edge of the clearing where he had his battle with the Achaeans. Just standing there and looking into space."

"I imagine he's thinking about the complications."

"But I thought Dryads had easy childbirths. My mother said I came in the time it takes a deer to wade across a small stream. The next day she was up and baking a woodpecker pie."

"I was thinking of political considerations. You know, Aeacus's brother hasn't any wife or children. That means that this baby of Kora's will be first in line for the throne of Knossos."

"Knossos will have to find another king," said Eunostos indignantly. "This baby's going to stay with Kora, and you know Kora can't leave the forest. She would die away from her tree."

"That's what I mean. Complications."

If Kora foresaw difficulties, she never admitted to them, though she spoke often of the child. On one particular day in early fall, when the vineyards were swollen with grapes and the Centaurs were setting their wicker vats on stools to prepare for the vintage, she sat at her loom and Eunostos held her yarn. Aeacus had gone to visit Chiron, with whom he had struck up a friendship, and left Eunostos to keep his wife company. But she was not spinning, she was talking. She always found more to say to Eunostos than to Aeacus. Since her marriage, she had grown surprisingly fond of small talk, all the little happenings in the forest which Eunostos and I saw or heard about from our friends. How the Bee Queen Amber had been sharply chastised by Chiron when she was apprehended in stolen sandals. How two more Bears of Artemis had joined Phlebas's herd and stealthily gathered weed in the forest by the light of the moon. Kora reserved her divinity for Aeacus. With Eunostos and me, she could show herself to be, as he had described her, familiar and pleasantly mundane like a hand loom. It was no wonder that she had trouble talking to Aeacus. After marriage, it is hard to be and at the same time talk with a dream.

She and Eunostos were discussing her child. "If it's a girl, I'm going to name her Thea for my great-grandmother. If it's a boy, his father will call him Icarus. It's a good family name among the Cretans." She had trained her hair to dip in curls over her forehead, the Cretan style, and covered her pointed ears.

"Why not have twins? Then you can use both names."

Kora laughed heartily. She often laughed with Eunostos. "One at a time, please. Can you see four of us in this tiny room? With just me here, Aeacus has to get off by himself sometimes."

"You could marry your mother to one of her suitors and get an extra room. By the way, I miss your ears."

"Aeacus says I'm more mysterious when I hide them. It leaves something to guess at. As for marrying mother, I'm afraid there's not much hope unless I can find a deaf Centaur."

"If you have two babies," said Eunostos, and Dryads often bore twins, "you could always give one to me."

"A bachelor with a baby? Eunostos, you wouldn't know what to feed him."

"I'd leave him with you till he was weaned. Then I'd feed him—well, the same as I eat. Fried sparrows. Woodpecker eggs. Weasel stew."

"He'd get a stomach ache and keep you awake all night with his crying."

"Then you tell me what to feed him. I'll make a list on a palm leaf."

"Eunostos, I believe you're serious."

"I am," he said shyly.

"You can be my baby's Zeus-father. How would you like that? You can help me look after him when"—and her voice quavered a little—"when Aeacus goes on his explorations."

After that, Eunostos told everybody that he was going to become a Zeus-father. He built another room onto his house ("for my Zeus-baby") and began to make toys instead of furniture in his workshop. Aeacus showed him how to make a toy glider out of willow rods, and Bion brought him some clay to model animals—bear and wolf and ibex—and with the help of Kora's loom he stitched a little pointed cap with a woodpecker's feather which he said should fit a girl as well as a boy. He much preferred a boy, since girls were too breakable, but wanted to be prepared for a disappointment.

Aeacus, on the other hand, was very quiet about his impending fatherhood. Everyone knew that he loved children, cubs, calves, anything small and helpless. In that respect he was like Eunostos. And no one doubted that he would like a child of his own—not even me, and I was never one to admire him. But somehow he seemed more troubled than expectant. I wondered if he really wanted his maiden, his goddess, to become a mother. Like her, he had loved an image, and now the image was about to change and grow maternal and divide the love she could give him. Also, when a man knows that he is free to leave a place and return to his own country he is often content to stay. But when he is bound by children as well as a wife, he may grow fretful and homesick. A Cretan prince reared in a palace was never intended to live in a forest with a green-haired family.

* * * *

It was a girl. Her name was Thea, as Kora had promised. Myrrha was so distraught that I had no trouble replacing her as midwife.

"Fancy being a grandmother," she kept sighing. "Do you think it will frighten off my suitors?" I insisted that she wait downstairs with Aeacus and Eunostos until I had bathed the child in myrrh-water and placed her in Kora's arms. Such a grave little face, looking at the new world and already making judgments! Dear Zeus, I thought. Not another silent one! At least she looks healthy.

"Come on up," I called down the ladder.

Eunostos and Aeacus clambered up the ladder, with Myrrha close behind them. At the last minute, Eunostos remembered that father and grandmother come before Zeus-father and waited his turn to greet the mother and child.

Kora smiled up happily from the couch as Aeacus scooped the girl in his arms. The delivery had been quick and almost painless for her.

"She has your mouth but my ears," she said proudly.

Bewilderment, quickly replaced with a smile, flickered across Aeacus's face, almost as if he had not expected a daughter with pointed ears and green hair. Almost as if he had fathered a kind of beautiful freak. Don't misunderstand me. He loved his daughter from the moment of her birth—more than he ever loved Kora—but I think that she made him feel the permanence of his exile from Knossos. By choice he had wed a Beast and settled among her people. But had he the right to rear his daughter as a Beast, in a tree instead of a palace? No poppy-shaped skirts for her, nor strolls beside the Great Green Sea with a saffron parasol nor an afternoon at the bull ring. She was born a princess; she could have become a queen, since women have often held the throne at Knossos. But here she was among beings with tails or hooves or pointed ears, and branded as one of them by her own ears. You understand that this is only a conjecture. Aeacus never confided in me. But Cretans are easier to fathom than Egyptians. They are sometimes subtle but rarely inscrutable. They sometimes smile when they wish to cry or nod when they disagree, but I could read Aeacus like a half-opened scroll.

Fortunately, no one else seemed to notice his hesitation. Eunostos and Myrrha were looking rapturously at the baby, a piquant creature in spite of her grave countenance, with generous green hair (but then, Dryad babies are never born hairless).

Eunostos could no longer remain in the background. "Let me hold her, Aeacus. Kora, can't I hold her? I won't drop her. I'm her Zeus-father, remember?" He cradled the child in his arms and the grave, troubled look left her face, and she began to smile. Who would have thought that such a big, rough-handed boy, without any brothers and sisters for practice, could have held a baby so gently that she would give her first smile?

"Sleep, little Thea," he whispered. "There won't be any Striges in your night. You have two fathers to look after you." Then he began to hum an old lullaby:

"Sleep, little Dryad, sleep in your tree.
Listen! The wind sings silverly."

Aeacus was not looking at his baby. He was looking at Eunostos, for the first time with unmistakable jealousy.

CHAPTER XI

TIME PASSED even in the timeless Country of the Beasts, though as imperceptibly as the dripping of a water clock. For three winters, snow fell on the mountaintops, melted with spring into a hundred silver freshets which cobwebbed the forest like a giant spider web, dried with summer to stream beds which grass and clover and violets hurried to green, as if dry beds had no place in so rich a country.

And there were changes among the Beasts. Eunostos was eighteen, a strapping young Minotaur who toiled from cock-crow to lamp-lighting time in his workshop but, I am pleased to say, resumed the wenching which his unfortunate courtship of Kora had interrupted. I myself had enjoyed six new lovers, five Centaurs and one precocious and surprisingly well-mannered Paniscus. And my tree, aside from looking a trifle scarred from the depredations of woodpeckers, thrust its vigorous limbs to the sunny skies and showed no signs of decay or decline. Bion had left his nest and come to work in Eunostos's workshop, where he labored at his own table and cut gemstones or embellished Eunostos's furniture with mosaics and intricate workings in copper and bronze. Only Partridge never seemed to change, the eternal adolescent, chewing his onion grass and trotting after Eunostos, who still loved him and pretended that he was the brightest chap in the country.

A second child, Icarus, had been born to Kora less than a year after the birth of Thea. Eunostos had asked to adopt him and, being refused, came even more frequently to visit at her tree. Kora's beauty was undiminished but different. There was a greater fullness to her body; her alabaster cheeks were faintly flushed, like roses reflected in snow. If mystery had gone from her, even for Aeacus, familiarity had given her a becoming softness, and she seemed indistinguishable from loom and cradle and brazier. As for Aeacus, he kept his own counsel. He still hunted with Eunostos, though not so often as in the early days. If he loved the maternal Kora less than he had loved the maiden, at least he was unfailingly courteous to her, and no one could question his love for his children, especially Thea, whom he adored with the adoration which he had once reserved for her mother. But his walks in the forest had become a frequent occurrence and I, for one, wished that one day he would keep on walking until he reached Knossos.

It was morning. Eunostos sat with Kora on the porch. Icarus and Thea lay side by side in a large cradle, a product of Eunostos's workshop. Eunostos was talking; at the same time he was gently rocking the cradle with his hoof and watching the babies with the corner of his eye. Icarus was gurgling happily, plump as a robin, but Thea was looking uncomfortable, if not quite disgruntled.

Eunostos was eating raisins in large handfuls and when Kora turned her head, he would slip a few to Icarus, who was not supposed to eat them, said Kora.

But Eunostos knew better, since his own mother had fed him raisins as soon as he was weaned. Thea, on the other hand, grimaced whenever he made her an offer.

"The Centaurs destroyed Phlebas's lodge yesterday," he said, sharing some news brought to him by Partridge. "They rowed out in a raft and threw torches onto the roof before the Panisci could get out their slingshots. Of course the lodge burned in a few minutes. All the Goat Boys and their Girls escaped, as the Centaurs intended, but they'll have to find a new place to keep their stolen goods now."

"It's high time," said Kora. "It was the dirtiest place you can imagine."

"I can imagine. I know Partridge," said Eunostos, "though," he hurried to add, "his dirt is honest."

Aeacus walked onto the porch in noiseless sandals. "I'm going to call on Chiron," he said without explanation. He was not rude; he was never rude. But there was something a little strained about his smile. Surely he isn't jealous of me after all this time, Eunostos thought. Perhaps he is just homesick for Knossos.

"Would you like to take Thea with you?" Kora asked.

"You know she's afraid of the forest."

"But she wouldn't be with you. At least not after the first few times. Do you realize she's never been further than Zoe's house in two years?"

"She's safer where she is." It was not that Aeacus considered her a burden who would spoil his walk. In the house, they were inseparable. It was almost as if he did not want her to know and love the forest.

He lifted her out of the cradle and laid her over his shoulder and patted her. She almost never laughed, but she seized him around the neck and hugged him, and looked displeased when she was returned to the cradle. Eunostos felt a lingering pang. Scarcely a month ago, she had come to him as soon as to her father, but all of a sudden she had begun to seem frightened of him. "Was it something I did?" he asked me. "It's only a phase," I reassured him, but I had a hunch that Aeacus, in his smooth Cretan way, had somehow turned her against Eunostos. Perhaps he had told her a story about a demon with horns and a tail and a red mane. At any rate, Icarus hugged Eunostos as often as he had the chance and clearly preferred him to his father. I wondered how soon Aeacus would start to tell him stories.

"Good-bye, little Thea," Aeacus said. "Rest well while I'm gone." Then, with a pat to Icarus's head and a kiss on Thea's cheek, and no farewell at all for Eunostos, he reentered the house to descend the ladder and waved to Kora from the ground. It's because he's so used to me, Eunostos told himself. I've become like a piece of furniture to him.

"Kora," said Eunostos suddenly. "Thea is nearly two, and she's never seen my house. Do you realize that every time I invited her, Aeacus thought of a reason why she should stay at home? For that matter, you and Icarus have stayed at home too much lately, too. If you aren't careful, you'll turn into a loom."

"I don't think Aeacus would like me to bring her," she said hesitantly.

"Well, why not? I'm Zeus-father to both children, and if I don't have a right to entertain them, I don't know who does. Remember, I built a special room for them. There are still toys in it—the ones I haven't brought over here."

"Aeacus seems to think that something might happen to Thea in the forest. He keeps bringing up the time I was kidnapped by Phlebas and sold to Saffron."

"Saffron is dead and Phlebas was so frightened by Chiron that I don't think he's much of a threat. Besides, there's some kind of danger everywhere, even here. Your tree might catch on fire."

"All right, we'll go!" she said with the sudden enthusiasm of someone about to be slightly mischievous. "We'll have a real outing. Which baby do you want to carry?"

"Icarus."

"Shame on you, Eunostos. You're partial."

"I love them the same," he said (and he did—well, almost— except that he was a little frightened of Thea since her estrangement from him). "But Icarus is easier to entertain. I can talk Beast to Beast with him. He understands me, you know, even if he can't answer. Though he did call me 'Zeus-father' yesterday."

"Eunostos, he was only gurgling! He can't even say 'mother' yet."

'Well, he can say 'Zeus-father.' I distinctly heard him. Anyway, he's too heavy for you to carry."

"Empty the arrows out of Aeacus's quiver and bring it along. Icarus likes to ride in it."

They set off together for Eunostos's house, with Icarus and quiver strapped to Eunostos's back, and Thea in her mother's arms. Icarus was so excited by the journey that he almost squirmed out of the quiver; he kept up a constant happy gurgle which Eunostos insisted contained several "Zeus-father's." Thea, however, began to look around her apprehensively the moment they left the tree and, when a Bear Girl scampered across their path, she set up a howl which she steadily increased until they reached Eunostos's stump. You would have thought that she was one of those superfluous girl-babies which the Achaeans abandon to the wolves. Only when she saw the inviting walls of bark, green with ivy and entered by a door like a big smile, did she subside, and once within the walls she managed a faint coo, which Eunostos dared to hope was directed to him. If I could bring her here often enough, he thought, she would stop being afraid of me.

"Oughtn't you to latch the gate behind us?" Kora asked.

"Oh, no, some of my friends might come to pick vegetables. I give them the run of the garden."

To roses and columbine he had added forget-me-nots, violets, and hyacinths; and his fruits and vegetables now included carrots, radishes, squashes, gourds, and even a grapevine with several succulent bunches. He had also planted three olive trees which eventually, he hoped, would supply him with oil. He had built an olive press in his workshop.

"One of these days you'll be completely self-sufficient," said Kora with admiration. "You'll grow and make everything you need. Eunostos, I'm proud of you."

"Three years ago, you said that carpentry wasn't very poetic," Eunostos reminded her.

"That was three years ago. Now I can see poetry in a well-made chair."

"I wish—" he began. But no, he must not express or even entertain such wishes. "Come into the house, Kora."

Icarus had visited the Zeus-father room on several occasions and he crawled at once to the toy glider, which he had already battered—broken a wing, bent the tail—but which remained his favorite toy. Thea, who could walk for short distances, headed for a doll of terra cotta, a little girl with round painted eyes and smiling mouth, who looked like a happy Thea. The resemblance was no accident; Eunostos had used her for his model. She sat in a corner and cradled the doll in her arms and looked at him for the first time in a month as if his horns were friendly instead of frightening.

With the children thus occupied, Eunostos invited Kora to walk into the garden. It never occurred to him that there might be danger in his own house.

"I want to ask you about one of my rose bushes." He led her among the flowers and indicated a particularly woebegone bush. "I water it every day and can't understand what's wrong."

"She isn't eating properly. You can get some potash from the Centaurs. To roses, it's what bread is to you and me."

"I knew you'd know. That's just what I'll do."

They strolled from the roses to the workshop and climbed down the ladder to greet Bion, who was polishing a large amethyst. He greeted them with a wave of his feelers but, dedicated worker that he was, never stopped the rapid swish-swish of his forelegs.

"We'd better get back to the children," said Kora. "Thea might get scared."

As they emerged from the workshop, they heard a whispering—not the children's—from the house.

They broke into a run.

"It's only a Bear Girl," said Eunostos with relief. "They're very gentle with children."

The Girl was cradling Thea in her arms and talking to her. She looked up at them, startled, and then she smiled, no more than a child herself. Her smile was engaging, but her fur was in need of a comb.

Kora darted across the room and snatched her daughter as

if from the jaws of a Hydra. Eunostos was about to defend the Girl, poor thing. The Bears of Artemis were always welcome at his house and free to pick his grapes. Often they came in his absence and left him pails of blackberries.

"It's one of Phlebas's Girls," explained Kora. "She's spruced herself a bit but I still recognize her after three years. You'd better see if anything is stolen."

Quick as a rabbit, the Girl shot out of the door. There was nothing in her paws and it seemed pointless to chase her, since she wore no garments in which to conceal any loot.

"Well, she would have stolen if we hadn't caught her," Kora said.

Eunostos was not sure. "I have an idea that with the lodge burned down, she just got homesick for her old way of life in the log village. She couldn't go back there—Phlebas's Girls are outlawed, you know—so she came here instead and found a baby and felt maternal."

"If she's the one I remember, she has a baby of her own, and it's a horrid little thief."

"Well, no harm done," he said. "But I expect we had better head back for your house."

They had hardly begun their walk, however, when they saw that Thea was not just quiet, she had fallen asleep, and she never slept during the day, least of all when she was being carried through the forest and had an excuse to wail. Furthermore, her face was flushed as if she had lain in the sun or caught a fever.

When they reached Kora's house, she had not so much as flickered her eyelids.

Aeacus was waiting at the head of the stairs in the trunk. He greeted them with his customary noncommittal smile and Eunostos wished for a scowl. It was what he deserved, he felt, for taking the children into the forest without their father's permission.

"Thea seems to be sick," he said quickly, to save Kora from

having to make the confession.

Aeacus took Thea out of Kora's arms and hurried her onto the porch and into the cradle. He fell to his knees and peered anxiously at her face. Then he placed his hand on her forehead.

"She's not hot. Are you sure she's sick?" he asked, looking more puzzled than angry. "She seems to be sleeping quite peacefully." In fact, to judge by her smile, she seemed to be having a euphoric dream.

"We can't wake her up," said Kora.

Puzzlement became alarm. "Eunostos, get Zoe."

Minutes later I too was kneeling beside the bed and since I have acquired certain medical skills through my long friendship with Chiron, I recognized the symptoms. In a way, Aeacus was right. She was not sick, she was drugged.

"Where has she been?" I asked. Eunostos told me about the outing and the Bear of Artemis he had found in his house.

"One of Phlebas's Girls, you say. Do you know what they do when they want their own babies to stop crying? They drug them. They give them a bit of weed to chew, or else they brew some in hot milk."

"But why would the Girl drug Thea?" Kora cried. "Was she going to kidnap her?"

"I don't think so. I think she probably came to steal from Eunostos. She had lost everything when the lodge burned down. She had heard how he leaves his gate unlocked and she just walked in, hoping to find him gone. She probably heard him with Kora and Bion down in the workshop but hoped she could come and loot and go before he came out. In the house, she found Thea, who was about to cry and give her away. So she quieted her with some weed. Then Eunostos and Kora surprised her and she pretended she was just rocking the baby in her arms."

"Will she be all right?" Aeacus demanded.

"Oh, yes, though she may act a little strange when she wakes up."

Thea's strangeness took the form of hilarity. She woke up giggling and giggled for almost an hour. Then she demanded dinner, ate like a hawk instead of a sparrow, and fell into a natural sleep. It had not, after all, been a tragedy, merely a mishap with certain amusing aspects. At least, that was how Eunostos saw the incident, and I had to nudge him when he started to suggest that they give Thea some weed every day. Kora sat on the floor rocking Thea's cradle and looked up at Aeacus with a smile as if to ask his forgiveness, but—at the same time—to say, It wasn't so bad after all, was it?

Aeacus did not return her smile.

"Thank you for coming, Zoe," he said, and then to Eunostos he said some words which were all the more terrible for being spoken with measured politeness and with an impassive face.

"Eunostos, you're not to come back for awhile."

Kora jumped to her feet. "But what has he done? He just wanted our children to see their toys. You ought to thank him!"

"For taking my daughter into the forest where she might have been killed?"

"But she's not even hurt."

"She might have been, though."

For once, Kora stood up to him. "Our daughter is a Dryad. She lives in a forest. She needs to get to know her own country. Do you think she can spend five hundred years in this tree?"

"No," he said. "I do not."

His words were cruelly prophetic.

CHAPTER XII

"ZOE!"

I muffled my ear with the corner of a wolfskin. It was early morning and I had scarcely fallen asleep after the departure of Moschus; wineskins littered the floor and wine cobwebbed my thoughts.

"Zoe, will you lower the ladder?"

I recognized Kora's voice. Anyone except Kora or Eunostos I would have ignored. I dragged myself from my womb of coverlets and staggered to the door.

"Yes, dear?" I felt like a Cretan feigning a smile when he wanted to frown.

"May I come up?"

She was laden with both of her children, Thea in her arms, Icarus in the quiver strapped to her back. She wore a russet gown embroidered with green clover leaves, and her smile was as radiant and natural as mine was forced.

I lowered the ladder; what is more, I forced myself to descend, rung after painful rung, and lift Thea from her arms. I felt my years when that little bud of a girl seemed as heavy as Icarus. Inside the house I hastily returned Thea to her mother and sprawled full-length on the couch. For once, Kora would have to guide the conversation. I hardly had energy to listen—until I heard her announcement.

"I'm going to visit Eunostos," she said as if such visits were a daily occurrence. "Since I can't carry both children all the way, I wondered if I could leave Thea with you."

"Do you think it's wise to call on Eunostos? After what Aeacus said?"

"Aeacus doesn't know. He's hunting again. Besides, it's mainly Thea he doesn't want carried about the forest."

"You know very well he doesn't want you to see Eunostos."

"I don't care." There was bronze in her voice. "Eunostos

wants to see me, doesn't he?"

"Of course he wants to see you." How could I explain that seeing her and Icarus so rarely and under surreptitious circumstances might hurt him more than seeing them not at all? He was trying his youthful best to build a life without her and his Zeus-children. In the past few weeks he had turned out a three-legged stool to rest my ankles, an olive press for Chiron, a slingshot for Partridge to defend himself against the rough Panisci, and endless other artifacts which he gave to his friends or traded to his acquaintances. Partridge had come to stay with him in the stump; Bion was already staying with him. He was seldom alone, rarely unoccupied, and only cheerless when he thought himself unobserved.

"It's just that—well, he's taken to wenching again, and it's good for him, and the sight of you might make him stop. You know what I say: 'A celibate Minotaur is a sick Minotaur.'"

"I'm glad," she said resolutely, though she looked more wistful than glad. "Is he—popular?"

"Sensational. As a stripling, he was always vigorous, but callow and inexperienced. Now my friends tell me he's become the ideal lover. He's added grace to vigor; he's learned how to pleasure a woman with all those sentimental endearments which make us feel loved as well as desired, if only for the evening. They say he's pleasured every Dryad between twelve and four hundred—except for a few stubbornly faithful wives in Centaur Town."

"And you, Zoe?"

I gave her a look which would have wilted the wings of a Bee queen. "You know he's always considered me his aunt."

"I'm sorry," she said quickly. "It's just that I know how—generous you are. Well, I'm sure my visit won't change his habits. It's Icarus I mainly want him to see. After all, he's the child's Zeus-father. And to tell the truth, I want Icarus to see him. You'd be amazed that such a little child could miss anyone so much."

"I wouldn't be amazed at all, when that someone is Eunostos. As a matter of fact, I've noticed that Icarus has looked a bit peaked for the last two months. Now he's not even gurgling. He looks almost like"—I started to say Thea. "Almost subdued. Yes, I'll keep Thea for you, but she's starting to look uncomfortable, as many times as she's been here."

"Tell her a story about the Bears of Artemis. The nice ones, not Phlebas's band. I won't be long."

"As long as you're going, you might as well stay awhile. Otherwise, you'll disappoint Eunostos." But she had already gone.

* * * *

She entered the gate, unlatched as usual, and paused before she lifted the door-hanging to his house. She wanted to see him entirely too much. Perhaps, she thought, if I turn very quietly and tiptoe out the gate—It was too late. Icarus emitted a happy chortle.

There was nothing to do but enter the room. Apparently Eunostos had been kneeling beside his fountain to feed his turtle, the one with which he had replaced his wedding present to Kora and Aeacus, but he was already on his hooves and starting for the door to meet her.

He had dropped a platter of baked flies in the water (he trapped them on parchment dipped in honey) and he looked at her and Icarus as if they had returned from an audience in the Underworld with the Griffin Judge.

"I couldn't bring both children," she explained. "Zoe is staying with Thea."

He lifted Icarus from the quiver and hugged him so tightly that she thought: he is going to break a rib.

But Icarus returned the hug with equal enthusiasm and refused to leave Eunostos's arms. For an instant she envied her child. There was such a wonderful reciprocity between him and Eunostos: a spontaneous and unstinting affection. And the thought, quickly erased from her mind, prodded her, goaded her: except for my dream, except for my dream... Now she did not even permit herself an embrace. It might be misunderstood; it might recall the rejected thought.

"It's been two months," she said. It was not a reproach—Aeacus after all was to blame—but a lament.

"And two days."

"Eunostos, let's sit in the garden. Did the rosebush grow after you fed it the potash?"

"It's the biggest in the garden now." He was patting Icarus and tousling his hair; at the same time he was staring at Kora with an ardor which he could no longer mask as brotherliness.

There were mossy chairs among the columbine, their legs entwined with creepers and looking as if they too might have grown in that garden of sweet familiarity. Side by side they sat in the sun-warm morning and the inarticulateness of their long separation was like a gate between them. Even Icarus seemed to feel their constraint and sighed in Eunostos's arms.

"Is it better in your tree now that I don't come? I mean—"

"You mean is Aeacus more content? I don't know, Eunostos. I don't think so. He doesn't talk to me very often. He smiles and nods and rocks Thea in her cradle and then goes hunting or to call on Chiron. Are you—are you happy with your girls?"

"Oh, I make do," he said, shuffling his hoof.

"Do you bring them here?"

"No." The answer was abrupt and decisive. "I built this house for you." He hesitated. "Do you still love him, Kora?"

"Yes. I want to be with him even when he's silent and I can't read his silence." It was true, in a way, and something else was also true. It was not meant to be spoken, but her tongue, silent too many years, betrayed her now. "But I love you too, and so do the children!"

"Icarus maybe."

"And Thea, if she only had the chance."

She took his hand. Such a big, rough hand, and yet what slender fingers he had! It was no wonder that he could make a poem out of wood, an elegy out of a chair or a toy. It was a sisterly gesture, she persuaded herself. She had not embraced him, this rough carpenter with the heart of a poet. She had never embraced him, even when he had rescued her from Saffron. But in this slight endearment she felt enfolded by all of his boyishness-turned-adult. For an instant—for more than an instant—she envied those light-headed, lighthearted Dryads who had enjoyed his more than brotherly kisses. It was all very well to love a dream; it was like drinking a great flagon of long-buried wine and feeling as if you could step from one treetop to the next. But then the sparkle and the lightness evaporated like dew on a maple leaf. To love a Minotaur was like eating a loaf of wheaten bread soaked with honey; there was no sparkle but there was a sweet and enduring nourishment.

"Icarus isn't a bit bigger," said Eunostos. "Oughtn't he to have grown in the last two months?"

"He doesn't eat as much as he did. He misses you. Now we have to go, Eunostos." She had already betrayed Aeacus with her thoughts; she must not risk a worse betrayal.

"No, please, I have to find a present for Icarus first." He clutched the child as if he were protecting him from a blast of wintry wind or a pack of wolves.

"He's had his present. Coming to see you. Now he wants to give you one."

Icarus held to Eunostos's horns and implanted a wet kiss on his cheek.

"When will you come again?" The question was addressed equally to her and Icarus.

"I don't know."

"When may I come to see you? Aeacus didn't say I could

never come again."

"I don't know that either, Eunostos."

He hurried into his workshop and returned with the feathered cap he had made for Thea, but made too large. But it fitted Icarus perfectly because of his hair, which doubled the size of his head.

Eunostos stood in the gate and waved his hand. Icarus waved his cap and then he began to cry. His mother hurried him into the trees. It was fortunate that she knew the trail so well; all the way home, she never looked up from the ground.

Aeacus had returned ahead of them. He was hanging his bow on the wall.

"I shot a bear," he said. "If you salt the meat, we can have steaks all winter."

"We don't eat bears in the Country of the Beasts."

"Suit yourself. Where have you been?"

"To visit Zoe."

"I see that Icarus has a new cap."

"Eunostos made it. He left it at Zoe's house."

Did he believe her? If he did not believe her, was he annoyed, angry, enraged? In all this time, she was still unable to penetrate his impassive smile. And yet she felt that in his strange, civilized fashion he still cared for her. It was not exactly love; it was the gentle and faintly condescending affection which sometimes survives the disappointment of losing a dream.

That night he lay beside her on their couch and held her hand and kissed her cheek.

"Kora," he said. "Maiden. You called to me across the dark spaces of the night and I came to you. Was I right to come? I'm still an invader, you know. I'm not a Beast."

"I wanted you to come."

"But are you still glad?"

"Yes, Aeacus." She answered without a pause but with a certainty which she did not feel.

"Then so am I. We have had good years. We mustn't regret them. And you have given me royal children."

He was quiet then. His hand relaxed its hold; he seemed to fall into a quiet sleep. She kissed his cool forehead, loving him in her way, though still not knowing him—this lover and stranger; but not, in spite of the vows he had sworn before Chiron, her husband—never truly her husband. Maiden had become wife and mother for a Man who had remained an alien and a wanderer.

She awoke to find him gone, and the children with him.

Luckily I found her before she had left her tree. I had been concerned about the consequences of her visit to Eunostos, though I had not anticipated quite so dire and sudden an outcome.

"It's a long way to Knossos," she said, "and I won't be able to carry much. A little food: a flask of wine and a cheese. And acorns to last me for a week." She had not been crying; she had not taken time for tears. She was not even angry. She was lost.

"It will take you three solid days to reach Knossos. You'll never find your children and get back to your tree alive!"

"I may overtake them on the way. He's burdened with the children."

"And if you do, how can you stop him?"

"I can't stop him but I can ask him to leave my children. Let him go, if he must, but leave my children."

"He won't listen to you. I won't let you go, Kora."

"You can easily stop me," she said. "You have the strength. But you will have to kill me. Will you do that, Zoe?"

I looked into her face and saw, for the first time, the utter implacability of a Dryad who had remained a girl too long and become a woman too quickly and meant what she said. I saw an unreasoning courage which, if rebuffed, might become madness.

"I'm going to get Eunostos," I said. "Wait for me till I bring him back. You can surely do that much for me. Together we'll think what to do."

"I can't wait."

"Ankles be damned," I swore, and ran like Artemis at the hunt—ran all the way to Eunostos's trunk and fell in a heap at his gate.

"Aeacus has taken the children."

"Where?" It was his only question. He did not seem surprised, but anguish lashed him like the branch of a fir tree. I expected him to scream.

"Toward Knossos," I said. "Go after her. I'll follow when I get my wind back."

I overtook them where the forest opens onto the field. At least Eunostos had held her until my arrival, but she was even now breaking free of him, a tall, resolute figure encumbered only with a wicker basket and striding toward the Country of Men.

"Listen," I shouted after her. "How do you think you can get to Knossos? You've never been out of the forest!" She paused until I caught up with her. She had no words for me, but I had made her think. "Do you know what the Cretan rustics say of Beasts? They fear and despise us. They frighten naughty children with stories about our cannibalism. They would capture or kill you."

Her face was that of a bewildered little girl. "I could hide my ears and hair," she protested. "Dirty my cheeks and pass for a peasant going to market."

"And die before you found your children. How long do you think you can live away from your tree?"

"But I'm not bound to a tree," cried Eunostos. "I can go anywhere. I'll get your children for you, Kora!"

"And how are you going to disguise yourself short of a funeral shroud? Horns on one end and hooves on the other! You sound like Partridge."

"I don't need a disguise. One good bellow will send those

rustics scurrying like Bear Girls chased by a bear."

"And if you get to Knossos?"

"The Cretans aren't monsters. Not the city folk, anyway. The king is said to be a fair-minded Man. I'll ask him to make Aeacus return the children."

"And you think he'll listen to you? His own brother's children, heirs to the throne?"

"I don't know. At least he might let them spend half the year with Kora. But we have to do something, don't we?"

"Yes, we do. We'll go together, Eunostos, you and I. I'll be the peasant, not Kora, and I'll find a way to smuggle you into the city. You're right, the king is fair. He will probably refuse you but I don't think he will harm you. If he does refuse, then it will be my turn to act. I won't ask, I will steal back what has been stolen."

"But they're my children," Kora cried. "You're making plans as if I didn't exist!"

"Kora," I reminded her. "I am approximately seventeen times your age. I can stay away from my tree a good two weeks without so much as getting a headache. What is more, I am something of a traveler. I have been to the coast with Achaeans and I took a short voyage on one of their ships. Once, I even dyed my hair with umber from the banks of the Beaver Lake, combed it over my ears, and went to Knossos with a Cretan sailor who had taken my fancy. For a solid week, he showed me around the city—taverns, bull ring, theater, palace, everything. I was downright faint before I got back to my tree, but I didn't regret a minute. There is no more to be said if you want your children back. Swallow your pride and turn their rescue over to experts."

Perhaps it was wicked of me to feel a strange exhilaration even while Kora was grieving for her lost children and I sincerely and deeply felt her loss. But then I never claimed to be the Great Mother. I was nothing but a free-living Dryad who loved an adventure, amorous or martial. And loved Eunostos.

And so I prepared for my greatest adventure with my greatest friend.

CHAPTER XIII

MOST OF THE Beasts had gathered at the edge of the forest to watch my departure. Chiron and his Centaurs, wives as well as husbands, had arrived en masse, with their beloved pigs hovering between their hooves; and the Bears of Artemis, forgetting their shyness, scurried around me in a frenzy of excitement and wanted me to add some berries, some honey, some catnip, to the already laden pouch suspended from my sash. There were others too: some thirty or more Dryads, who took turns trying to reassure Kora that Icarus and Thea, having a human father, would not suffer even if separated indefinitely from their tree; the better behaved Panisci, among them Partridge, who was close to tears because Eunostos was going to the Wicked City without him; the Bee Queen Amber, who had made a special contribution to my pouch; and of course Eunostos, flanked by his faithful Bion and three other Telchins. Phlebas and his band were conspicuously absent, and his special Girl, chomping insolently on a weed, had been heard to say that she hoped the children—spoiled things—were *never* recovered; it would serve them right to be eaten by the Knossians.

As for myself, I had stayed in my tree all night to absorb its vitalizing powers, which now permeated my body like a glow of wine, and to make my plans and preparations. I could not have slept even if I had taken the time.

Now I was ready. It was not a small thing to leave the Country of the Beasts. I had left in the past only when accompanied by one of my lovers and returned with depleted energy, even if enriched experience. It was not a small thing to leave my oak. There were wispy little oaks in the world of Cretans but they were not Dryad trees and who could say what small sustenance I might draw from them?

Kora separated herself from the band of Dryads and threw her arms around me. Her eyes were moist but she did not allow the tears to fall down her cheeks.

"It seems I'm one of those women to whom things happen. You're one who makes things happen. Find my children for me, Zoe." She looked incredibly pale and young; she was both the devoted mother, inseparable from hearth and loom, and the dreamer of the early days, though now bereft of her dream. The sight of her briefly sobered me from the intoxication of the adventure.

"I will, Kora," I swore. "By the Great Mother's breast, I will." Confidence returned to me, and I felt that there was nothing in the forest or in the city which I could not accomplish, except become a fine, proper lady (or be loved by the one dearest to me).

Eunostos said nothing. There was nothing he needed to say. His smile said: "You and I, Aunt Zoe, who can stop us? Not those puny Cretans." He planned to follow and overtake me that very night.

I held him by the horns—the intimate, loving gesture shown him in the past only by his mother, Kora, and little Icarus—and kissed his cheek.

"Be cautious. I don't need to tell you to be courageous."

And then I left the country, marching out into the meadow where Aeacus, three years ago, had fought his battle. The grass was soft beneath my sandals; butterflies, like winged buttercups, fluttered away from me and meadowed the air. It is a good omen, I thought. The air has partaken of earth, and earth is my friend.

Omens can be deceptive.

*   *   *   *

I approached the farmhouse feeling—trepidation, did you expect me to say? Caution, perhaps? I refuse to be falsely modest. I approached with the complete assurance that I would get what I wanted, by wiles or sheer animal appeal, from the farmer:

the stone-wheeled oxcart in which he carried his produce to Knossos and in which I would hide the undisguisable immensity of Eunostos. Of course I knew my limitations. Place me beside Kora and I was clay beside alabaster. But Cretan farmers were not acquainted with women like Kora. I glittered, I glistened, I rippled like a snake goddess in a breast-revealing gown which my Cretan lover had bought for me in Knossos. Compared to the average, woolen-garbed farmwife, I was a finely glazed cup beside a crude earthenware jug. I was, to be frank, sufficient to fill a farmer's eye and make him drop his hoe.

This particular farmer was chopping wood with the rhythmic, leisurely motion of a man who had never known a bad harvest—not on rich Crete—or confronted Achaean marauders. His cart leaned against the blue, almost windowless thatched mud box which passed rather prettily for a house. His ox grazed in a neighboring pasture bosomed with hay ricks and besprinkled with daisies. Immediate theft was out of the question. Nor could I wait until night and make off with ox and cart without arousing either the farmer or the inevitable watchdog found in peasant homes. Cretan farmers are as wary as Bee queens, though for different reasons. They eat well on the fat of the land, but they own few possessions and guard them with a zeal enforced by pitchforks, hoes, and knives, to say nothing of dogs whose immediate ancestors roamed the forests and held their own with wolves. I must bide my time; I must wait till night, when Eunostos could creep out of the forest, some three miles away, and join me outside this very house. Meanwhile, however, I must beguile and ingratiate—and incapacitate the farmer and whatever family and animals he might possess.

He looked at me and dropped his ax. Evidently I had filled his eye, and his nostrils too, for he sniffed greedily at the myrrh in which I had bathed my face and breasts. He also looked at me with suspicion: what was this ample, not young but decidedly not superannuated woman doing in a bell-shaped skirt embroidered with conch shells and starfish and, boldness of boldness, in an open bodice which revealed, nay, accentuated and framed her two glories, her glowing pomegranates, her full moons, their nipples painted a titillating crimson to match her lips? Furthermore, I had ripped the gown in order to suggest an escape from bandits who had attempted my honor, and I had ripped in provocative places—a lure of thigh, a tantalization of leg. My hair, though brown with umber, scintillated with mica dust; my ears were concealed—at least their pointed tips—but the lobes were graced by big silver earrings, a loan from Amber, shaped like beehives and tinkling when I walked as if their inhabitants were about to take flight. I had touched enough kohl to my eyes and carmine to my cheeks to make me look not quite a courtesan, but at least a woman of experience, not a great lady but definitely not a peasant—perhaps a merchant's wife whose husband was often at sea; in short, a woman with a roving eye and the wherewithal to rove.

The farmer grinned and gaped. He was sleek and just short of being plump, since the Cretan countryside was luxuriant enough to support its farmers without wearing them to the bone. He wore an unembroidered loincloth which reached almost to his knees and over which his bare stomach had started to bulge. Give him a year, perhaps two, and he would become fat. As I approached his house I affected a limp and slyly observed him slyly observing the undulation of my bosom. He sucked in his stomach. Thus diminished, he was not unattractive and I vowed that if necessary I would sacrifice my rarest possession to secure the oxcart.

"Achaean raiders," I said in a throaty whisper. "I was going to visit my cousin in Gournia. Carriage stolen. Slaves killed. Wandering since dawn." I swayed toward him and he extended a steadying hand which lit on my shoulder but gradually crept toward my twin glories.

"Where?" The tone was peremptory; the speaker, his wife.

She had not so much emerged from the house as flurried; a little, swallowlike woman with a blackbird's voice. The steadying hand was arrested in its descent.

"Where did they attack you?" I paused to fathom her curious accent. The "you" resembled an "e." (Cretan peasants take enormous liberties with pronouns, but I will regularize them for the sake of my scroll.)

"Three or four miles from here. Over that hill—" I swept expansively with my hand to include the whole horizon and at least a dozen hills. I could not be specific since all I knew of the terrain was the general direction of Knossos. "But they've gone back toward the coast to their ships. No danger to you."

Apparently he was having similar troubles understanding me. Beasts and Cretans share the same tongue but not the same inflections. There is a certain huskiness in the voice of a Beast, whether Dryad or Minotaur, a lilt in the voice of a Cretan.

"Needs some beer, Chloe," said the husband at last, frowning at his wife and guiding me through the door. She returned his frown—for even peasant women stand up to their men on Crete—and followed us into the house.

The house was a single room, a hearth in the middle of the floor with an unlit fire whose smoke would have to escape from the one window, a pallet of straw, a low table without chairs, and an outsized and surprisingly clean pig. No, not surprising, since pigs like cleanliness; if they dwell in filth it is the fault of their masters. There was also a wooden cupboard from which the wife reluctantly drew a sheepskin of beer. I will have to say that in spite of the sparseness of furnishing, there was not a mote of dust, not a smudge of smoke. What is more, the cupboard was painted like a rainbow shell and graced with a single plain but exquisitely wrought cup of Kamares ware. But this was Crete, where even the peasants have a passion for cleanliness and an eye for color.

"I can't pay you," I said. "They took everything." Chloe's

frown intensified to a scowl. If she had the delicate frame of a bird, she also had the beady, incriminating eyes and, one guessed, the claws. She stared at my large leather pouch, which looked heavy enough to contain gold and jewels.

"Except my earrings," I added. "It nearly cost me my honor protecting them." I cast a quick, knowing look at the farmer, as if to say: Not that my honor is unassailable. That was my problem: to allure him and lull her. "They're real silver. Very old. Egyptian. I was born in Egypt, you see." Since I did not speak like a Knossian, I had to account for what must seem to them a foreign accent. I unfastened the earrings and presented them to the woman.

"Fetch her some cheese, Tychon," she piped in a much kindlier voice, a blackbird turned swallow. "Who're we not to show hospitality to the poor dear?" She was already inserting the bars of the earrings into her own pierced ears. They were so large in proportion to so small a woman that they brushed her shoulders, but she peered at her reflection in the side of a bronze kettle and seemed to find them becoming, for she gave her hair a quick sweep and looked at her husband with the expectation of a compliment.

"Charming," I said, trying to direct his attention from me to her. "Aren't they?"

"Yus." He was still looking at me, as if he wished to return the earrings to their original ears.

"He don't talk much," she said. "Do you think, ma'am, that—?" She pointed to her gray, shapeless gown of lamb's wool, more exactly to the part which concealed her breasts and, indeed, raised the question if she had any breasts to conceal.

"I think," I said, "that you could billow the sleeves a bit and cut away the front down to here—"

Her husband's pronouncement was terse but final. "Nope."

The swallow reverted to blackbird. "Ain't as if I were flat."

"Git supper for the lady."

Petulantly she began her preparations, but her petulance was directed at her husband, not at me. Now I was receiving covert looks from her as well as him. His said: "Style's fine for you, not her." Hers said: "Men got no taste for the new styles."

Supper, if not sumptuous, was clean and nourishing. Wheaten bread without worms or mold, fresh goat's cheese, peppercorns, and carobs from a tree in the yard. As I ate, I saw that both of my hosts, as well as the pig, were staring at me with unabashed fascination. My beauty, it would seem, appealed to the farmer, my gift to his wife, and my scent of myrrh to the pig. But all three stares asked the same question: What did I want besides a meal and a temporary place to rest? Was Tychon going to be asked to drive me into town in his oxcart? Was Chloe going to be asked to put me up until I could send for friends to fetch me home? Was Bottom going to eat less heartily with an additional mouth to feed?

"If I could just stay the night with you... I don't even need a pallet; I'll be on my way tomorrow."

"Walkin'?"

"I like to walk."

"All the way to Knossos?"

"I'll rise early and no doubt meet a farmer bound for market."

"I could drive you."

I forestalled a screech from Chloe. "I wouldn't think of it. You have your duties here on the farm. Besides, your wife is far too lovely to be left alone when there's even the slightest risk of Achaean raiders." (Not for nothing had I been captive to a deceitful Bee queen.) "They would steal her away to the mainland with them."

"Pass the beer to the lady, Tychon. And give a swig to Bottom."

I put my lips to the mouth of the skin (actually a leg, which served as the spout) and smacked with excessive pleasure. The beer was at least palatable. I had tasted worse at Moschus's table.

"An excellent beer," I exclaimed while Tychon dangled the leg above the snout of his pig.

"Made it hisself," the woman volunteered, fondling her new earrings and giving him a final chance, half plea, half command, to compliment them.

"Nice."

Her hand moved questioningly toward her breasts. "Nope. Some things is best left indoors." It was his longest communication.

The moment seemed propitious for my next move. Thievery, I was learning, could be fun. No wonder the Bee queens cultivated the art.

"And there's something else I managed to save," I said, reaching into my pouch, which was made of the sturdiest leather; though perforated with tiny holes, and drew out two—Striges! Yes, I had borrowed them from Amber, she who had been apprehended in the theft of sandals and chastised by Chiron. Now she was eager to appease him, and of course she knew that he and I were old and devoted friends.

"By the navel of Mother Earth," swore Chloe. "What be they?"

"Pets." I said. "Gentle, docile, and very affectionate. Let me show you."

They exchanged glances as if to say, "We'll be on our guard, but what's the harm?" and reluctantly permitted me to coil a Strige around each of their necks.

Tychon grinned and relaxed his stomach.

"Tickles."

If he looked a little less like a sheep, I thought, I could forgive the bulge. After all, I myself am not exactly a sapling, in age or girth.

"Looks like a bit of fur," said the wife, gazing at her reflection in the side of the pot to evaluate the combination of neckpiece and earrings and liking what she saw. You may give me credit for introducing a new feature of feminine adornment, though in later years ladies preferred their neckpieces to be inanimate.

Tychon yawned.

"Hoed too much," Chloe volunteered. "Ain't a boy. Tychon! Let her have the pallet." But Tychon had already sprawled on his bed of straw and begun to snore.

She shrugged. "Works hard, sleeps hard. Never mind. Don't talk much when he's awake."

I saw that we were headed for an exchange of confidences. I would no doubt be questioned about the fashions of the town, the affairs of the court. Drawing on my past visit to Knossos and what I had learned from Aeacus, I had prepared answers for all possible questions, even down to the false rumor of an indiscretion between the king and the wife of the Egyptian pharaoh's emissary.

But she pointed to my breasts and said, "Paint your nipples, dear?"

"Always. Whoever said we can't improve on nature? An unpainted nipple is like a green apple. Unappetizing."

"What do you use?"

"Carmine."

"Too dear for me."

"Had you thought of a vegetable dye? I've even made do with the juice of wild strawberries."

But she had slid as quietly to the floor as an empty gown sliding from a wall hook.

Remembering my own unpleasant experience with those pernicious creatures, I removed the Striges before they had glutted themselves and returned them to my pouch. Then I turned to the business at hand. I could not resist a smile. Zoe, old girl, I told myself, you're going to keep your promise to Kora.

Darkness came as stealthily as a member of Phlebas's band bent on theft, and I felt in league with the night, bent upon my own machinations, however benign, and hugely enjoying the adventure in spite of the hazards and the stakes. With a certain reluctance, I exchanged my elaborate gown for a shapeless gray horror which I found, of all places, in the cupboard. Now I could approach Knossos driving an oxcart and looking like a peasant woman and Chloe could mend a few tears and have a fashionable gown which for better or worse would liberate what her husband preferred to remain in captivity. Then I knelt beside Chloe to recover the earrings. Had they belonged to me, I would gladly have left them in exchange for the oxcart, but the Bee queen had lent, not given, and I must return them to her along with the Striges (which I would have liked to strangle).

However, I had underestimated the pig.

He bared his tusks and instantly transformed himself from a docile pet to a ferocious guard. In the forest, he could have passed for a wild boar. I understood why Tychon did not need a watchdog. Bottom advanced upon me with cautious but deliberate steps. Doubtless he was still making up his mind whether to gore me or ram me. Hastily I sprang to my feet. Chloe could keep the earrings so long as I got the cart. At the moment, the getting seemed in doubt. It was out of the question to implant a Strige on the back of that advancing brute. If I could only think of a bribe—

I had just seen Bottom partake of the family skin with some relish. I hastily emptied the rest of the skin into a pot, the same which had served Chloe for a mirror, and shoved it under his snout.

A moment of indecision. Was I really a threat? After all, I had left a better gown for the one I had taken and I had not stolen the earrings, merely fingered them. Furthermore, there was no reason to connect me with the sudden but not unnatural-looking sleep of his master and mistress. He sniffed, examined, partook: daintily at first, then mightily. I edged toward the door;

Bottom stopped lapping. It seemed that I was still suspect. I paused. Bottom resumed his lapping.

A drunken pig is far more fastidious than, say, a drunken Moschus. Bottom finished the bowl, walked without staggering to his master's pallet, leaned comfortably against Tychon, and joined his snores to those of his master. Fighting down the temptation to recover the earrings and risk arousing Bottom—later I could make amends to Amber—I moved out of the house to claim the cart and ox.

The ox was tethered under the lean-to beside the house. When I untethered him, he refused to budge. I coaxed, I prodded, I swore twenty oaths to the Great Mother, but I could not move him from the house. I felt like a beaver which has found a tree impervious to its teeth or, to use a comparison more fitting to my race, like a transplanted oak which has failed to take root in rocky soil.

To compound my disgrace Eunostos at that very moment loomed over the horizon, stooping and trying to minimize his almost seven feet but still looking like a Minotaur or, to the country folk if they had seen him, a demon from the Underworld.

"But Zoe," he cried, "you only have to talk to him." He turned to the ox, muttered a few, to me, unintelligible sounds, and the stupid animal sauntered, yes, sauntered, in spite of his bulk and with undisguised scorn for me and affection for Eunostos, from under the lean-to and over to the cart, which leaned against another wall of the house. A few more words, some quick, sure movements of his hands, and ox was joined to cart for the journey to Knossos.

"What did you say to him, Eunostos?"

"I invited him to join us on a trip."

"But he's going to have to pull us. You make it sound as if he's going to ride in the cart."

"I know, but he has his pride. It's better to make him feel like an equal."

"I didn't know you spoke ox."

"You forget I have an affinity for the race. I expect we have a common ancestor. Besides, his vocabulary is limited—a mere hundred or so words."

"Eunostos, you're a wonder."

He gave me an impulsive hug. "Aunt Zoe, you're the wonder. The way you handled the farmer!"

I shushed him with a finger. "And his wife and pig. But they may wake up. Into the cart with you now."

"Can't I drive while it's dark?"

"Not even while it's dark."

"But the farmers are all asleep."

"But not their sons and daughters."

It was like squeezing a Triton into a lobster box.

"Leave me a breathing hole," he pleaded as he lay on his back, knees drawn up, arms pressed against his sides, chin on chest.

I shoveled hay over him. "It's only a foot deep over your head. I have to hide your horns. You won't suffocate." It was no time to pamper him. "Just don't sneeze," I cautioned with a last toss of the pitchfork. Then I mounted the driver's seat and addressed the ox:

"Ho there, fellow, off to Knossos."

The ox refused to respond.

"My good Beast, let's be on our way!"

His inertia bordered on insolence.

A sound filtered through the straw, rather like a series of grunts.

"That's the most primitive language I ever heard," I snorted. "And he's not my equal, even if I did call him Beast."

But the cart began to move.

CHAPTER XIV

WE HAD driven our oxcart for three days and lived on blackberries and mushrooms and crayfish caught in streams swollen by the melting snows from the mountains. Once I inveigled goat's milk and eggs from a credulous farmer's wife, who took me for a widow light in the head, while Eunostos remained in his crypt of hay. Every night, when we stopped to rest and my body seemed one intolerable ache from the jolts of the oxcart, I ate of the acorns in my pouch and scarcely thought of my tree. With the resilience of youth, Eunostos unbent himself and slept soundly under the cart, his horns and hooves concealed by straw or wrapped in old strips of linen torn from the folds of the gown I had borrowed from Chloe. The last night before Knossos, I waited among the papyrus stalks and watched for intruders while he swam in a pool and cleansed himself from the journey, and then I took his place in the sweet-chilling water, though careful to guard my hair and not expose the forbidden Dryad's green.

I dare not call it a happy time, while childless Kora waited in the Country of the Beasts, her strained white face a spectre in our minds. But the plans, the risk, the hope—and hope seemed almost a certainty while we were on the move—bound us together with the comradeship of soldiers sharing danger, and also with the tenderness only possible between a boy and a woman who might have been his mother (or except accident of years, his beloved).

The morning of the fourth day, Knossos spread incredibly below us.

"Eunostos," I called down to him. "We're there. But we mustn't be seen together. When we reach the marketplace, I'll leave the cart. Give me a few minutes before you show yourself. Then you know what to do."

His head erupted from the straw. "It's like a rainbow fallen out of the sky!"

I submerged the head and the incriminating horns. "Not yet, simpleton. But yes, it is, and it looks as if it might return to the clouds at any minute." I blinked my eyes. It was not a city, it was witchery, and at such a time I could not afford to be bewitched. As an antidote to sheer, open-mouthed wonderment, I reminded myself that, according to my Cretan lover, the Egyptians did not approve of Knossos. Streets which meandered when they ought to advance. End beams projecting from houses as if the builders had forgotten them and wandered off to make love. Flat roofs unexpectedly bulging into impertinent attics. Story built upon story like so many afterthoughts. Little blue huts side by side with scarlet villas. Sprawling apartments whose windows were filled with fiery orange parchment. Such a riot of colors— garishness, said the Egyptians. Where was the dignity of grays and browns, of sand colors, pyramid colors? Such a want of planning. Wastefulness, said the Egyptians. Where was the grandeur of temples with pylon gates and obelisks as straight as the shaft of a spear?

But the Cretans laughed and made no excuses for their fallen rainbow. "You say we squander our colors. Look at a field in spring. Do the flowers offend your eyes, whatever hues they mingle? You say we build crookedly. Look at the forest. Do the trees grow in rows? Do the branches make perfect spheres above their trunks? Beside, we did not build our city, Zeus built it. When he was a little boy, the Great Mother said to him, 'You're restless, my son, on the mountaintop. Descend into the valley and build me a town to delight my heart.' And the child took stone from the mountain, clay from the banks of a stream, wood from the fir tree; and he snatched a whole rainbow right out of the sky and went into the valley without a plan in his quick little brain, but with a vision, and built his town in a single morning. And the Great Mother said, 'But the streets are crooked.' And the child answered, 'So is a stream,' and his mother smiled."

"Zoe, I thought we were almost there. I'm about to sneeze."

"We are I said, prodding the ox, who had finally learned to obey my commands. "I was just catching my breath. But now to practical matters."

Knossos alone among the great cities of Men was totally unfortified; its walls were its bull-prowed ships. But though there were neither forts nor gates nor even guards, except for the palace garrison, it was understood that farmers would not enter the city with their carts, or warriors with their chariots. The farmers marketed their grapes, olive oil, melons—whatever the season's crop—in a large open field flanked by vineyards and olive groves, or walked into the city to make purchases in the canvas-covered stalls, which fluttered like big butterflies, or in the arcades of shops, whose bare-breasted proprietresses were as pert and impudent as their pottery and figurines. In the absence of the farmers, no one bothered their carts, for theft belonged to the countryside, not to Knossos. It was not a virtuous city by any means: its consumption of beer and wine was legendary, its sexual practices imaginative and prodigious; but its sins (said the Egyptians), or rather its pleasures (said the Knossians), lay in partaking, not in taking. As they approached the city, the peasants somehow forgot their wariness and relaxed in a beneficent glow of brotherly and other kinds of love. Oh, they would bargain and haggle over a price, raise their voices even scowl on occasion—but to steal in Knossos? Unthinkable. There were no watchdogs, or dogs of any kind, only Egyptian cats, snoozing on rooftops or walking the clean unlittered streets as if they felt no yearning for their original homeland. For cats, like Cretans, abhor rules.

Great ladies and gentlemen traveled the meandering roads in sedan chairs carried by servants or slaves, but everyone else walked, for it was not a vast metropolis, like Babylon, but a relatively small city with small buildings for small people, and unwieldy wagons or clattering chariots were as unthinkable as elephants in a vineyard.

I had parked the wagon at the edge of the field, in the shade of an olive tree, since poor Eunostos must be roasting under his straw blanket.

"I'm going now, Eunostos," I whispered, standing by the ox as if I were talking to him like a farmer who dotes on his animal. No one was close enough to catch my exact words. "But I'll be watching you from a distance. Once you enter the palace, I'll go to the agreed spot and wait till lamp-lighting time. If you don't come, I'll assume they have captured you and do what I can to set you free. If you do come—"

"It will be with the children. Or else the children will come without me. And if they do, you must get them right back to the country and not try to rescue me. Promise, Zoe?"

I promised but whispered under my breath, "Mother Goddess, I didn't promise by you."

I sauntered casually away from the cart and mingled with a group of peasants, nodding and smiling but careful not to speak and betray my Bestial accent. Everybody else seemed to be talking, buyers to sellers, sellers to buyers. But suddenly the talk began to subside and then there was not a sound in all that crowd. It was like the wind leaving a field of barley and letting the stalks ripple into silence. Eunostos had climbed from the cart. I watched him as he shook himself free of the straw and started for the cobbled road which led through the field and directly to the palace. They won't harm him here in the shadow of the city, I thought, not even the superstitious country folk. Still, they will fear him and some will make sport of him.

I was mistaken. They stared with awe rather than fear at this seven-foot, horned, tailed demon who had materialized—from a cart, was it? More likely from the air! They did not throw rocks, they did not ridicule, they parted to let him pass, as if it were his city to which they had come, and where they remained by his sufferance. Perhaps because of his boldness—perhaps because he somehow glowed with divinity—they took him for a god instead of a demon. Now he had reached the road to the palace. Now he was overtaking peasants bound for audience with the king, and meeting ladies and gentlemen bound in the opposite direction for the market place. Voices lilted from curtained sedan chairs, the bearers halted, the curtains opened, and bare-breasted ladies dangled out of the windows. Children gathered on rooftops, pointing, gesticulating, but not ridiculing, and a small boy cried in a high, sweet voice.

"Mama, is it a Minotaur?"

"Yes, son. It may be the last Minotaur."

"Has he come to hurt us?"

"I think this one has come to bring us luck. You see, he is like the god we worship. The same noble horns!"

Looking straight ahead of him, never stumbling, holding himself at his full height, his red mane a splendor of silk and sun, his horns like potent but unthreatening weapons, Eunostos entered the stepped portico of the palace and mounted toward the gate. He did not need a forest to give him dignity. He brought the forest with him and walked in the courage of his purpose. Guards advanced to meet him, not to capture but to escort, and together they vanished between the red, down-tapering columns and into the palace of Minos and his brother Aeacus and the royal children, Thea and Icarus.

*   *   *   *

Eunostos was afraid. He felt as if he were drowning in a vat of honey. Beauty too beautiful. Softness too soft. Not even a hint of menace behind a smile, as in a Bee queen's face. He could have fought monsters, certainly soldiers; young though he was and, so he thought, ineloquent, he could have argued against wrath or cunning. But this implacable gentleness, this tyranny of softness. It was beyond him and he was baffled. The rainbow city, its toy people, and now, here, the little king with his triple-plumed headdress, seated on his gypsum throne and flanked by two stone griffins who looked as august but unmenacing as the frescoed griffins—green, red, and blue—which shared the walls with reeds and water birds. Where were the spears to bar his path? These slim-waisted boys who passed for guards—no older than himself—why, he would scatter them with one sweep of his arm! Besides, they were guiding, not guarding him. He might have been a visiting ambassador.

The king was holding court and granting audiences. Peasants mingled with courtiers; the raw sweet smell of earth with nard and sandarac. Everyone equal now before the king and come to plead his case, present his gift, ask his boon. Eunostos paused in the rear of the room. His hooves seemed made of bronze. His head spun with a bewilderment of colors and costumes. The men in their loincloths were bright and trim, but not particularly variegated except that here was a cloth which reached to the knees, and there was one which covered no more than the name implied; here was the wool of a peasant, there was the linen of a courtier. But the women... There were skirts like bells, skirts like upturned saffron crocuses, skirts like crowns with many tiers, and here was a lady in—what was the word? Not even Men wore them, except in parts of the East. Trousers!

The king smiled and motioned him at once to advance to the throne, between the throngs of petitioners on foot and spectators lounging on stone benches which ran the length of the walls. Eunostos did not flinch. He knelt before the throne as I had instructed him and waited to be recognized.

"Arise and be heard."

"I have come from the Country of the Beasts," he said.

"I know, my son." Minos was a young-faced king with hair as white as foam. What strange bird—phoenix perhaps—had given him the plumes for his headdress? What fishers had dived among coral and anemones and gathered the murex shells to empurple his loincloth? Bracelets of lapis lazuli; a necklace of coral like a strand of sea horses. Female adornments, but the

Man was anything but feminine. Eunostos liked him. He is more than Aeacus, more than any of his people, he thought. Stronger yet kinder. Once his wounds had healed, he would not have stayed in the Country of the Beasts to steal the heart of a Dryad. Had he stayed, he would not have forsaken her.

"And you are Eunostos, the last Minotaur. My brother has told me about you. You were his friend. I have sent for him now."

Aeacus entered the room without surprise and walked to meet Eunostos without hesitation. They might have been meeting to hunt together as in the old days. In the forest, he had been a beautiful alien. Here, he was beautiful, but intimately at home with dolphin-dancing walls and dolphin-gay people. He wore no adornment except a silver fillet in his hair. He needed no adornment, with his body richer than bronze, with hair like shadows caught in a loom and woven to intricate strands. Eunostos keenly felt his own dishevelment. His gray loincloth of homespun wool. The wisps of hay clinging to his arms and legs. And his hooves, his poor ridiculous hooves which no sandals in the world could hide. Yet no one had laughed at him, and even Aeacus looked at him with a kind of grudging and, at least to Eunostos, unaccountable wonder.

Aeacus extended his hand in the remembered gesture of fellowship. Eunostos did not return the gesture. The beautiful ones, the hurtful ones, he thought. Kora and Aeacus. They smile and their enemies drop their daggers or lose their hearts. They can only be wounded by others like themselves. And I, in my roughness and plainness have dared to tread in the very fount of beauty.

Almost furtively Aeacus dropped his hand. Almost too quickly, he spoke. "I did love your friend, Eunostos. I do love her, in my way. But I love my children more. Would you deny them—this?" He swept his hand in a circle around the room, but the circle seemed ever-widening—palace beyond room, city beyond palace, island beyond city. The Minoan Empire, athwart the sea like an ocean-shouldering whale (and no one yet knew how close were the deadly sharks).

"Can't they have both?" Eunostos cried. "The forest and the city?" His cry was sulphur in the honied air. "Kora is lost. I think she will die without her children."

"She has her friends, Eunostos. You and Zoe and the rest. Good friends. I would have brought her gladly to Knossos. But she would have died in the city, away from her tree. You know that better than I. Had there been no children, I would never have left her. But there are two, and both are royal. Do you really think I can send them back to a forest of wolves and goat-footed thieves and kidnapping queens?"

"Is that how you saw the forest? Is that all you saw?" It was at once an accusation and a lament.

"Not you, not you, Eunostos. I liked you from that first day when you wanted to heal my wounds. I never stopped liking you, even when I forbade you my house."

"It's true I love Kora. But I couldn't have taken her from you. I would never have tried."

"It wasn't Kora I was afraid of losing to you."

"Not Kora?"

"It was my children. My son, at least. In fact I have already lost him. Now I must do my best to win him back. To teach him to rule a kingdom. It was you I feared, Eunostos, because the longer he knew you the more impossible it would have been for me ever to have taken him from the forest. And that's why he mustn't go back with you."

"But you can't be afraid of me," Eunostos protested. "I'm just a rough carpenter who stumbles over his own hooves."

"Who is wild and yet gentle, free and yet bound by the bronze ties of love, and binding to those who meet him. There are two forests, Eunostos. I feared—a little—the forest of wolves and thieves. But yours—and you—struck terror to my heart. The first was a danger I knew how to fight. The second was a magic against which I had no defense except flight."

"I didn't mean to make you afraid. I hope Icarus loves me, but I never thought about taking him away from you, his own father. I never thought anyone would love me as much as they loved you. Kora couldn't."

"Even Kora returned to you at the last. In her heart, I mean. So you see I'm not really forsaking her. I'm leaving her with you."

Aeacus was befuddling him with these strange compliments. Who could believe the Man? Lyre-tongued Aeacus, no doubt with another lie!

He turned to the king with a last desperate plea. "The Achaeans have a goddess, haven't they, who was stolen by the lord of the Underworld. Not the kindly Griffin Judge, but a cruel tyrant called Hades. Her mother—whether she was the same as our Great Mother I don't know—grieved for her and wandered over the world in search of her, and Zeus felt pity and returned the girl to the surface for half of every year.

"Even in the Country of the Beasts, we know you as a fair-minded king. You deliver justice to peasants as well as court-iers. What about Beasts? Our races were friendly, long ago. I don't know what divided us. Reunite us now! Become our Zeus, great King. Let Kora have her children for half of every year. The Great Mother will thank you for it."

Minos was slow to answer. He was not Aeacus. Words did not come glibly to his tongue. "But the goddess you speak of was stolen by a strange god. A father can hardly be accused of stealing his own children. These are my heirs, Eunostos. You see me enthroned in splendor. You've heard of my fleet which holds the Achaeans at bay. We are friendly with Egypt, unthreatened by decadent Babylon. My ships have sailed beyond the Misty Isles, and around that great dark island to the south. What you see and think and hear is the truth. For now. This cubit in time called now. It is true that I am great in wealth, powerful with ships. But power is no more constant than the rain. Inevitably there must come a drought. I must conjure the rain. I must fight to retain my power and leave it in fitting hands. My brother has spoken truly, though he was very wrong to wed your friend. Kora must suffer so that a great empire shall be justly ruled. Icarus and Thea must be taught to rule, you see, not to run wild and free in a forest as most of us would like to do. Do you think I want to sit on this throne and pretend to be a god, and condemn this man and praise that man, and order my ships into battle? No, Eunostos. I would much rather go hunting with you in your forest and drink beer with your friend Zoe and join Chiron on his travels. But I follow the will of the Goddess because she has marked me—both honored and cursed—to be a king."

"But there are two heirs. Can't I take one of them back to their mother? At least for a little while?"

"There are two of them now, but will both grow up to rule? The Great Mother sends death even to laughing Knossos. Pestilence comes with our returning ships; the winter wind blows cold from the north. I myself was stricken as a child. A demon of plague denied me the power to beget children. He might as easily have killed me. No, my son. Both children must remain in Knossos."

This, then, was the ultimate anguish: that Minos was just. Eunostos knew that in the king's place he would have delivered the same judgment.

But he could fight that judgment. His allies were hope and courage and, much to his surprise, a wiliness which would have done credit to a Bee queen.

"May I see the children to say good-bye?" How easy it was to lie for Kora's sake! He did not even feel shame and no one appeared to notice what this hitherto guileless rustic had learned from the Cretans.

Aeacus's smile darkened. "What good will it do, Eunostos?

Icarus cries for you every day, as it is. If he sees you again, he will have to get used to losing you again."

"At least I can tell their mother if they're well. She thought they might sicken when taken from their tree."

"She needn't have been concerned. Chiron himself assured me that they could live without their tree, though of course he never suspected what I had in mind."

"Yes, you may see them, Eunostos." It was the king. It was a command.

Aeacus turned to him with a flush of anger. "My brother—"

Minos was quick to forestall him. "Eunostos has risked his life to bring these children back to their mother. The Great Mother, I think, would wish him a final visit with them. In our household shrine, we worship her son in the form of a bull. Eunostos is closer to divinity than you and I."

"May I see them in your garden with the pool of silver fish?"

Aeacus forgot to be angry. "You remembered my telling you about it? And that was three years ago!"

"You played there as a boy. It sounded so beautiful that I wanted to see it. And I want to see the children out-of-doors, not under a roof. For a little it will be almost like the forest again."

*　*　*　*

He waited beside the pool. The silver fish idled among conch shells and coral. Blue lotuses languished in the bright sun, like maidens weary from the heat who had waded into the pool. Palm trees imported from Libya, and oleanders tapering their long green leaves from clusters of white and pink blossoms, and grapevines climbing trellises against the wall, and a single blue monkey scampering among the flowers with the insolence of possession: here was Kora's dream, Aeacus's truth.

Aeacus walked into the garden carrying Icarus and leading Thea by the hand. There were no guards with him. There seemed no need for guards, since the wall was too high to climb. Thea withdrew her hand and boldly approached Eunostos. Out of the forest, she did not seem to fear him. Perhaps, he thought, she remembers that only for a little while I seemed to her a horned demon. Perhaps she remembers me, at the first and at the last, as one who loved her.

She did not hug him but she smiled with a wise little smile and touched his hand.

He patted her hair; by accident, he brushed a curl away from a pointed ear. She carefully rearranged the curl and then returned to her father.

Icarus, meanwhile, seemed to be struggling out of sleep. He blinked his eyes, which were red as if from prolonged weeping. Then he recognized Eunostos. When he yelled, the blue monkey hid among the oleanders and the silver fish scattered among the conch shells.

He lunged from his father's arms and Eunostos caught him and fell to his knees, laughing, and hugged him with wordless yearning, and loved him for Kora's sake and as if he were his own son.

"Talk to him, Eunostos. Try to make him understand why he must stay here with me. He loves you best, I know that. But he must stay with me."

"I don't think he understands many of my words."

"You don't need words. You never did."

Aeacus turned abruptly and walked into the palace with Thea, and Eunostos called after him. "Wait. Can't she stay too?" But the mouth of the door was dark and silent. He knew that he had lost her, and the loss was as bitter as aconite, but Thea had never loved the forest. It was only fair, however painful for Kora, that one child should stay with her father and grow to become a queen.

Now he must act to save Icarus. Now there was no time for words, except to allay the suspicion of whatever guards might wait beyond the door.

"There ought to be a turtle," he said. "Shall we go and look for one among the grapevines?"

Icarus nodded agreement—he would probably have nodded if Eunostos had said, "Shall I throw you into the pool?"—and Eunostos walked quietly to the far wall and prodded among the grapevines with his hoof, lifting, twisting, exposing. Yes, it remained, the old fissure through which Aeacus's turtle had escaped into an adjacent courtyard opening onto a little-used street, and which Aeacus had never allowed to be filled with rubble or clay. Hastily Eunostos parted the vines to enlarge the opening. Small, small, but just large enough for Icarus, in spite of his hair.

"Zoe," he whispered.

"Yes, Eunostos. I'm here at the other end. The courtyard's empty. No one can see me from the street."

"Thea isn't coming. Call to Icarus."

"Icarus, it's your Aunt Zoe."

"Go to her, Icarus." Will you follow me? the child seemed to ask.

"Yes, I'll follow you." He kissed him on his green profusion of hair and thrust him as far into the opening as his hands could reach. It was the only lie he had ever told the boy. Even in happy Knossos there must be prisons for those who helped to kidnap a prince's son. Probably there were executions. Never mind, if Zoe escaped from the city with Icarus.

He had just risen to his feet and walked to the pool when Aeacus returned.

"But you just left him," Eunostos said calmly. "We were playing hide-and-seek. He's hidden himself among the oleanders."

"Call him then. You had best be starting back to the forest. Kora should know as soon as possible how things are. Tell her— tell her that she is still my Maiden."

"I'll tell her."

"But where is Icarus?" Aeacus strode through the garden looking behind the bushes.

"He can't have gone far, can he? There's no way out of the garden except through that door. Or you wouldn't have left me alone with him."

"Except—" Aeacus stared at the torn vines against the wall. "You remember more than I thought. Guards!"

The garden was suddenly aswarm with lithe young Cretans, faces taut, hands on daggers.

"My son has been stolen by—who was it, Eunostos? Who came with you and waited beyond the wall?"

"I came by myself."

"I don't believe you. You love Icarus too much to thrust him out into the city alone. It can't have been Kora. She couldn't have made the journey. It was Zoe, wasn't it? Yes, it must have been. She would have both the courage and the strength." And he gave a hurried description to the guards. "Rather large. Handsome in a weathered kind of way. Hair probably dyed or concealed. No doubt dressed like a peasant. She will have hidden Icarus under her robe. Alert the garrison. Let no one leave the city."

But there must be a thousand women in Knossos who fitted such a description, and the city had no walls and a very small garrison. Zoe indeed had courage and strength. And roads, crowded with carts and asses and oxen and peasants, led in many directions.

But then the cry, the beloved and shattering cry. "Zeus-father!"

Icarus returned through the fissure into the garden, laughing and scrambling toward Eunostos but at the same time inevitably, irrevocably, it seemed, away from him and toward the griffin-flanked throne of Knossos.

CHAPTER XV

WE RODE IN silence, Eunostos and I in the same farmer's cart which had brought us to Knossos, but flanked now by six Cretan horsemen astride Hittite chargers. It was no longer necessary to conceal Eunostos under the straw. The whole countryside knew of the Minotaur and the Dryad who had come to Knossos to steal Aeacus's children and how they had been imprisoned for seven days until the king had decreed, against the protests of Aeacus, their return to the forest. We were not criminals, be had said; we had come to reclaim a mother's children and, according to our own law, come with a just cause. But Cretan justice required that if we ever returned to Knossos, we would face imprisonment and death.

Eunostos had not reproached me for letting Icarus slip from my arms and return through the fissure into the garden.

"I hid him under my robe," I had shamefacedly explained. "And held him against my side. But before I had even reached the street, he slipped out of my grasp. He was frightened of the dark, I expect, and he wanted you." I did not explain what I did not wish to believe, that perhaps I had somehow willed him to escape, unconsciously relaxed my hold to keep from having to leave the city without Eunostos. I had hoped, I had dared to hope, that the King would give both of the children to Eunostos—or give him a promise of their later return—and that he would bring them to me in the deserted courtyard and we would return together to Kora. But when Icarus scrambled out of the fissure and Eunostos whispered, "Thea isn't coming," I knew that Eunostos would have to stay in the palace and I would gladly, though not deliberately, have exchanged Icarus for my beloved friend. But I did not reproach myself. Icarus had returned for love of Eunostos. Perhaps I had let him return for the same reason. One must make allowances for love.

"You may go now," said the captain of the horsemen, a little man with the tiniest ears I had ever seen, almost like coquina shells, riding a large and indelicate animal who endured his rider with the same disdain which my ox showed to me. From the distance, you might have mistaken horse and rider for a Centaur. All six horsemen watched while we climbed out of the cart and crossed the last small space of meadow, and the captain called after us.

"Is it happy in the forest? With the Dryads, I mean, and houses in treetops, and workshops under the ground? After seeing you, I think it must be a magic place!"

"I don't know about the magic," said Eunostos. "To us, it's just home. But it certainly used to be happy. I wish you could visit us, but Chiron wouldn't allow it. Thank you, sir, for bringing us here. You'll return the ox to his owner, won't you?"

"I won't forget. And I wish you had gotten the children!" He reined his horse and gruffly ordered his men to return to Knossos by way of Tychon's farmhouse.

"Eunostos," I said. "I'm very tired. I've been two weeks away from my tree. Seven days without acorns. I'll have to rest before we visit Kora."

He looked at me with concern, his young face a mixture of tiredness and tenderness. He had rarely heard me complain. "Of course, Aunt Zoe."

"Eunostos, Zoe, where are the children?" It was Partridge. "I've come here every day to watch for you." He dropped his onion grass and threw his arms around Eunostos. "What happened in Knossos?"

"We didn't get them," Eunostos said, returning the hug wearily but gratefully. "The king wouldn't let them go. They have to stay with their father and learn how to rule a kingdom."

"Never mind, you still have me."

"Yes, old friend, I still have you. I'm glad you waited for me. I'm taking Zoe to her tree now. We'll visit later. You and I and Bion. I'll tell you everything."

I was so fatigued that I had to lean on Eunostos for support. I felt as if a Strige had supped on my blood. My hands were sweating and my hair clung in damp tendrils around my ears.

"As soon as you get me to my tree, you go on ahead to tell Kora."

"Yes, Zoe."

He helped me up my ladder and onto my couch and threw a wolfskin over my now shivering limbs. I thought of course that he would go without me. I must have fallen asleep. I awoke in perhaps an hour. Already the emanations of the tree had revived my body, if not my spirits. Eunostos was still sitting beside my couch.

"I told you to go on," I said. "Kora has to know, and you were the one to tell her. She may have heard the news from Partridge."

"I didn't want to leave you that long. You looked so feverish! And then you started to have chills. But you seem better now. Here, eat some of these acorns."

He had lit a fire in my brazier—he must have borrowed some coals from one of my neighbors—and roasted the acorns while I slept.

"I'll eat them on the way."

"You're sure you're strong enough?"

"Of course I am! It wasn't a fever I had, it was what we call tree-sickness. Besides, it's only a few hundred yards to Kora's oak."

He helped me down the ladder as if I were an old lady and I became increasingly impatient with him, though my impatience was really to be finished with the intolerable duty of facing Kora. How do you tell a mother that she has lost her children?

It was when we entered the meadow that we saw the smoke. We broke into a run.

The trunk of Kora's tree was sheathed in flames and the

limbs were writhing arms of fire. For an instant it seemed to me that the tree itself was Kora. I thought I saw her face contorted in the blaze of foliage; I thought I heard her crying, but it was only the thin, eerie whistle of burning wood.

Others had arrived ahead of us: Partridge and Bion and a host of Dryads, and Myrrha, who, we later learned, had just returned from a visit to the Centaurs, and thus had been gone from the tree when it caught on fire. Eunostos plunged toward that deadly pyre of flame.

"No!" The voice was like a bee sting to the ear. It was the usually soft-spoken Myrrha. "No, Eunostos."

He stopped in his tracks and listened without taking his eyes from the burning tree.

"The tree is stricken. Kora is dead or dying. Even if you carry her out of the flames, you will only prolong her agony. Allow her the dignity of dying as she chooses." I would never again mistake her for a foolish, light-headed woman.

He stared from Myrrha to the tree. A branch crackled and fell to the ground and Partridge stamped on the sparks in a frenzy to be of help. The tree was a single quivering flame. Mercifully, there was no sound in the trunk, not the least sob. Silent Kora did not break her silence.

"Don't you understand? It was Kora who lit the fire. It was not an accident."

Eunostos sank to his knees, his hands outstretched as if he could somehow conjure the flames to die or Kora to live. Partridge ran to him and said, "I told her, Eunostos. It was my fault. I didn't want you to have to tell her. It was my fault."

"It was nobody's fault," I said to Partridge. "Somebody had to tell her. Go to Myrrha and take her to stay with the Centaurs. I'll look after Eunostos."

For the last time I looked at the tree. Again I seemed to be looking at Kora; but she was dressed in the colors of autumn instead of her familiar green, and tranquil, strangely tranquil, yielding the summer without regret. Fearless of winter. Foreseeing the fadeless asphodels of the Underworld.

* * * *

Eunostos disappeared to his limestone cave. I did not try to stop him. Bion took hickory nuts, Partridge took onion grass and tried to cheer him with the news of the forest: Phlebas's quarrel with Amber over a theft, Myrrha's move to an oak near Centaur Town. I visited him every day with a pail of milk—he refused beer—and sometimes sat with him. He would not have heard me if I had spoken. He would have nodded; he might have smiled; but his mind was in the meadows of irrecoverable youth, the yellow gagea of unreturning spring. Those strong, practical creatures, the Minotaurs, carpenters and craftsmen and farmers…how rarely do we remember that they are also poets. And it is the inescapable burden of poets to forget that there are summers as well as springs.

Then, at the end of three days, he came to me, a tired, bespattered figure dusty with limestone, cockle-burrs in his mane, and sank to the floor. I sat on the couch and smoothed his mane with a wooden comb (he did not approve of my tortoiseshell comb; shells should remain on tortoises, he insisted).

"Aunt Zoe, was there ever a time when you lost everything?"

"There have been times when I thought I had."

"But I know I have. I could have learned to live without Kora. I already had, in a way. One day I may be able to accept her death, since she wanted to die. But the children. Icarus…"

"You're quite sure you're never going to fall in love again? You're only eighteen. What about the next five hundred years?"

"Almost nineteen. Yes, quite sure. Three years ago, I was happy, Aunt Zoe. So happy! I thought I had everything I wanted, except my parents, and I knew they were safe in the Underworld."

"It isn't in the scheme of the Great Mother for us to have

everything we want. If we did we wouldn't need her, and even a goddess likes to be needed. The lucky ones among us get half. But reach high, and half is enough. Now I sound like Moschus when he's drunk too much beer and thinks he's a philosopher. But I do know this. You haven't lost everything. You still have your friends. Don't forget them."

"But Kora and the children…"

"Kora is dead. You can't resurrect her from the Underworld, but you can be sure that the Griffin Judge has judged her kindly. I think that world is lovelier for this world's loss. And her children are alive and loved by their father and uncle."

"But I can never see them again."

"Never? Oh, my friend, that is a word for cynics. I don't pretend to be a prophetess. But like most of my race, I can sometimes catch glimmerings of the future. And I hope—I think—you will see your children again. Last night I had a dream. My soul went out of my body, as Kora's used to do, but it wandered in the future, not the present. And I saw a young girl—oh, how beautiful—and a boy with a crown of green hair, and where do you think I saw them?"

"Where?"

"A great bird was carrying them through the sky and right toward this forest!"

"But that was only a dream. If I try to go to them, Minos will have me killed."

"But they were coming to you. Kora dreamed of a prince and called him into the forest. It's true he brought her sorrow. But the fact remains that he came. Keep on loving Thea and Icarus and perhaps they will hear you. Remember, the forest is in their blood. It is half of them. Perhaps it will call to them too."

"I'm not Kora. I can't live on a dream."

"And you shouldn't. If I have any wisdom at all, it is this: dreams by themselves are for children. But if you dream and reach and wait all at the same time, then pygmies can topple giants, cities can rise from rubble! Strong hands and a dream and patience built Babylon, and it wasn't really Zeus who built Knossos."

I ran my hand through his soft-as-milkweed mane and held him by the horns and kissed him on his smooth face, almost the only part of his without hair.

"I'm not good for much, Eunostos. Beauty I had, and maybe there's a little left, if you don't mind a few wrinkles. Wisdom—I leave that to Chiron. But if you ever want to cry, this is the place to come."

"I'm not worth your love, Zoe. I'm nothing but the last Minotaur—and maybe it's just as well."

"The last—or the best?"

He laid his head in my lap. Then he looked up at me, with those unbearable green eyes which windowed his soul, and said, "Zoe, I know you've loved a lot of Beasts and Men and gotten over them. But was there ever anyone you loved more than the rest? And lost him? And thought you were going to die?"

"Yes, Eunostos. Though I can't say I lost him since I never really had him."

"I can't imagine anyone not loving you."

"He did, I think, in his way. But not in my way."

"What did you do?"

"Ached, my dear, and baked a weasel pie!"

"And did you finally forget him?"

"I didn't want to forget him. He was much too precious to me. I just rearranged my memory. Forgot some things, remembered others."

"I can't do that."

"You'll learn in the next hundred years or so."

"And you aren't sorry?"

"Not for a moment. I haven't regretted any of my loves.

Least of all the one that hurt the most."

"Will you tell me who he was?"

"Someday, my dear."

AUTHOR'S NOTE

If there were not a sequel to *The Forest of Forever* called *Day of the Minotaur*, in which Eunostos is reunited with his children, I would never have concluded this book with such unrelieved gloom. Unhappy endings are sometimes demanded by the Muse, but unnecessary unhappy ones are anathema to her—and to me. I would probably have burned up Kora all the same; I never forgave her, the foolish girl, for rejecting Eunostos in favor of Aeacus. But I would certainly have allowed Eunostos to smuggle Icarus back to the forest.

However, there is a sequel. Zoe's dream, even to the "great bird," was truly prophetic—and Eunostos, who reaches high, gets more than half of what he wants.

I should add that for reasons known only to my Muse, the sequel was written before *The Forest of Forever*, which as Bob Roehm and Alexis Gilliland (those two fine fanzine editors) suggested, might therefore be called a prequel; and there are discrepancies between the two books, for which I apologize and which I will correct if there is ever a second edition of *Day of the Minotaur*.

I refuse to apologize for writing a second book about the same characters, though I know the enormous risk of disappointing those who liked the first. Really, though, I had no choice. Eunostos came to me in a dream and said, "You didn't tell everything the first time. You didn't tell enough about Zoe."

Who am I to quarrel with a Minotaur?